NO CHOICE AT ALL

DENISE CARBO

Editing Contributors: Jami Nord and Dayna Reidenover

❀ Created with Vellum

This book is dedicated to my son, Jared. He's my own gentle giant with a heart of gold.

CHAPTER 1

"*M*orning, killer."

My ankle wobbles and my heel catches on the seam in the sidewalk. I glance between my coffee and the concrete. Which should I save—my dignity and possibly some scrapes and bruises or the specialty coffee I've been dreaming of all morning and finally indulged in?

A muscular arm slips around my waist and steadies me while a tanned hand whips the cup out of my fingers. I slap my palm against a solid chest covered in black cashmere and glare up at Ian Flannigan's smirking face. He pulls me flush against his body.

I try not to notice how all our key parts line up perfectly as I jerk out of his hold. He lets me go, but his hand squeezes my hip first.

"Must you persist in that ridiculous nickname? I dispatched one spider. You act as if I murdered a colony of rabbits or something."

"It's the way you got rid of the spider. You brandished your shoe like a serial killer in a horror film wielding an axe."

I roll my eyes. So sue me, I don't like spiders.

"And that's not why I call you killer."

I narrow my eyes. Do I want to know? Probably not. It's bound to ruin my mood for the rest of the day. Ian gets way too much enjoyment out of pushing my buttons. The sad fact is I know this, yet I still can't help reacting when he does it.

His sea-blue eyes stare down at me, patiently waiting for me to ask. They're not your typical blue eyes. Oh, no. They're the color of the Caribbean Sea—turquoise one minute and a deep blue the next. It's really not fair for him to have eyes like that. Or the long black lashes framing them.

"Never mind. I don't want to know."

I step to the side. I'll walk around him—ignoring Ian often works best.

He side steps in front of me.

"Where are you off to in such a hurry? Your flower shop is that way." He points behind me. "Or are you so flustered by my presence you've forgotten where it is?"

I close my eyes and start counting. *One. Two. Three.*

"Fantasizing what I look like naked?"

His tan, naked, chest with a sprinkling of dark hair pops into my head. My fingertips tracing each ridge of muscle on his abdomen.

My eyes pop open. *Damn it!*

I growl and stomp past him, muttering, "I have the worst taste in men."

He falls into step next to me. "So you admit you're attracted to me."

Do not engage. Do not engage.

I increase my stride. If I ignore him, he might give up. At least for today. Then he'll start over the next time I have the misfortune to run into him.

His long legs easily keep pace with mine. I slow down. It's not like I can win a race with him in this skirt and heels, and I'm sure as hell not going to give him the impression I'm running away from him.

"So, Becks…"

I stop and wave my finger under his nose. "Do not call me that. Ever!"

One imperious deep brown eyebrow shoots up.

Shit! I just gave him ammunition. Now that's probably all he'll ever call me.

"Got it. Rebecca it is."

He looks sincere. He could be setting me up, but his telltale smirk is missing. I spot my coffee cup still in his grip.

"Give me that." He holds it up over my head when I reach for it. I could snag it out of his hand, but then my coffee would spill.

I plant my fists on my hips. "What are you, five?"

There's the smirk.

"It's a little late to be asking how old I am, isn't it? You've already had your way with me."

Only a handful of people are strolling along the sidewalk, and they're too far away to hear him. Hoods and hats cover several heads, hiding identities and muffling sound further. No one glances in our direction.

I adjust the strap of my purse on my shoulder and fold my arms under my chest. His gaze drops to my cleavage.

"Eyes up, Flannigan."

He grins as he raises his gaze. "Can you blame me? Especially when I'm aware of what's under all that camouflage?"

"What camouflage?" I glance down at my white silk blouse under my wool blazer and the gray pencil skirt covering me to my ankles. There's nothing wrong with the way I'm dressed. It's tasteful and professional. The April weather is still rather brisk, but this is New England. It could change in an instant. My wool suit seemed like a good choice this morning, but I hadn't anticipated sprinting down the sidewalk to avoid Ian, either.

He steps closer. "Tell me, you're wearing sexy lingerie under those clothes, aren't you? White lace? A thong?"

I grit my teeth. Nailed it on both counts. Lingerie is my weakness.

"You will never find out."

His gaze rakes me from head to toe. "That's okay. I have my memories to sustain me. For now."

A shiver skates down my spine. Me too.

Nope, not going there. "Hand over my coffee."

"Have dinner with me."

"No."

"Why? It's just dinner. You're not dating anyone else. What's the harm?"

I tilt my head to the side and tap my toes inside my shoes. "How do you know I'm not dating anyone?"

His smile fades. "Are you?"

I should tell him yes. Only, then I'd have to come up with someone because Ian will insist on knowing who. He doesn't have a shy bone in his body. Why should he? He's probably had women falling at his feet since he left the cradle. He's just too damn good-looking.

"I don't date."

"Why not?"

"That's none of your business. You asked. I said no. That's how our little drama works, isn't it? Now can I please have my coffee? I have an appointment."

He hands me my coffee. "Here you go, Queenie."

"Let me guess, as in Queen Bitch?" He wouldn't be the first.

"I would never call you that."

"Why not? I know I'm a bitch. I don't see it as a terrible thing." My mouth waters as I inhale the nutty aroma of the coffee safely back in my grasp.

"My mother would smack the back of my head if she ever heard me call a woman a bitch. Besides, I don't think of you that way at all. You're determined to resist my charming personality, but you aren't nasty about it."

I narrow my eyes. "That can change." I guess I have to be harsher in my rejections of his advances. Good to know.

He chuckles and slides his hands into his pants' pockets. The gray material pulls against his thighs. I snap my gaze back up to his face.

"Queenie was this Boston Terrier I had as a kid. She would bark and growl at any dog that came near her."

"You're comparing me to a dog." And here I thought the day couldn't go worse.

Ian smirks. "She was a great dog."

"Uh-huh. Goodbye."

I look both ways before stepping off the curb onto the crosswalk.

Granite Cove doesn't have any traffic lights in this part of the village. During the summer, the locals avoid driving down Main Street when it's jampacked with tourists and summer residents. Otherwise, it can take a half hour just to traverse the half mile through the village with all the stops to let people cross. It provides good business for me and the rest of the shops located here, though.

Ian steps onto the opposite curb with me. I look up the street to his bar. That might be his destination instead of following me, but Flannigan's Pub is on the opposite side of the street. He should have crossed at the last crosswalk. Now he'll have to walk past his bar to the next crosswalk.

"Are you following me?" Go ahead, deny it.

"Yup."

I stop, turn to face him, and take a sip of my coffee, not caring if it's still too hot and burns my tongue. I need the caffeine kick. The late morning sun shines in my eyes as I squint up at him.

"Why?"

"You admitted you're attracted to me, so you've strengthened my resolve. My persistence will pay off. You're going to say yes eventually. So why not save us both some time and say yes now?"

"I say 'I have terrible taste in men' and you translate it as 'I'm attracted to you'?"

His lips twitch. "Pretty much."

I roll my eyes and stalk down the sidewalk. He's never going to stop. Is he right? Will I eventually give in? I grit my teeth and swing around.

He's only a step behind me.

I wave my coffee in the air with my finger pointed in his direction. "Listen closely. You were a mistake. I don't repeat my mistakes. I learn from them. Leave me alone."

Ian frowns and leans his head down so his nose is almost touching mine. "You know why I call you killer? It's short for man-killer. Have a nice day, Rebecca."

He crosses the road even though the closest crosswalk is half a block away. His posture is stiff instead of his usual casual strut.

I bet he thinks I'm a bitch now.

Mission accomplished. He won't be asking me out anymore, and I won't be tempted to say yes.

I sip my coffee as I stride over to Dress to Impress and swing open the door. The doorbell chimes a fairy tales trill.

"Right on time."

Kelly dresses a mannequin in the window display. She glances out the window and back at me. "Everything okay?"

How much did she witness? I point to the blue dress she's draping. "That's gorgeous. One of yours?"

She stares at me for a moment. The debate she's waging whether to press for details or allow me to change the subject is clear by her slightly wrinkled forehead, narrowed eyes, and pursed pink lips.

"Yes, as a matter of fact, it is." She steps down and walks over.

"What are you doing here in New Hampshire? Why aren't you a famous fashion designer in New York or Paris?"

"I did my stint in both and couldn't cut it. This suits me better."

I glance back at the dress in the window. The stitching is invisible. The material shimmers. I can easily picture a model wearing it strutting down the runway.

"You're so talented. I believe you can succeed anywhere you want to."

She presses the tips of her fingers against my forearm. "Thanks, but Dress to Impress is all I need. It satisfies my creative outlet, and I get to buy beautiful clothes to sell as well."

"I do love coming in here. Every time I do, I see so many things I want to try on."

"That's exactly the point."

I laugh as I follow her to the rear of the store, past rack after rack of beautiful clothes. There's a circular raised platform in the center. Thick white curtains drape over the dressing rooms on the left side of the room. A white and gold loveseat and chairs occupy the right side.

"You've really got a 'fairy tale princess' vibe going back here. I like it."

Kelly glances over her shoulder. "I have a weakness for fairy tales, and what bride doesn't want to feel like a princess on her special day? Or a teenager going to prom? Or even dressing up for a special dinner and wanting the perfect dress? I kept the decor simpler in the front so the clothes are the chief attraction, but back here I indulged."

"It works." There's a tall golden urn on a pedestal in the corner. "You know, hydrangeas and some long grasses would look great in that urn. We could do silk if you don't want the expense of replacing them often."

"That would be great. Can you work up a proposal for me?"

"Absolutely."

"I have your bridesmaid dress hanging in here." She stops next to an open dressing room. The light blue dress fills the entire lower half of the cream wall.

"Did it get bigger?"

Kelly laughs and glances at the dress. "No, but it will once you put it on with the train and puffed sleeves."

"Lord, when I told Franny she should have her dream wedding and not worry about finding bridesmaid dresses we could wear again, I never envisioned this would be the result." At first, she had insisted the bridesmaids all choose their own dresses as long as they were the same shade of blue. Sky blue like the eyes of Mitch, her fiancé. But Lucinda knew Franny wanted to recreate a wedding set at the turn of the nineteenth century. Sisterly love or the job of the wedding planner slash maid of honor? Either way, once she'd told Olivia and me what Franny really wanted, we could hardly refuse. After all, it's the responsibility of the bridesmaids to help ensure the bride's special day is perfect.

I step into the dressing area and set my purse on the white corner shelf.

"I'll take that." Kelly removes the coffee cup from my hand. "You'll get it back after you try on the dress."

I frown and snatch back the cup and chug the rest. "There, the dress is safe."

She shakes her head and takes the cup I hold out. The rings at the top of the curtains rattle against the gold-colored metal rod holding them up as she slides them closed.

I'm down to my skivvies and pulling on the special slip when a throat clears outside the dressing area.

"So, now that I know you're not going to bolt, what is the deal with you and Ian? No one can miss the bantering between you two at the business meetings, and I saw you talking to him outside."

I pause mid-step with the slip half on. Kelly and I are what I'd call friendly acquaintances. I like her well enough, but I'm not ready to divulge all the sordid details of my relationship with Ian Flannigan.

"Nothing to tell." If I didn't believe attending the town's small business group meetings was so vital to my business, I would've quit the first time I'd walked in the door and spotted Ian. I'd nearly fallen on my ass. I'd grabbed the door frame of the conference room and was on the verge of hyperventilating. I'm sure my eyes had bugged out of my face like a cartoon character while I debated if it was too late to move back to New York. His gaze had landed on me and widened with recognition. When he grinned, I'd let go of the door, raised my chin, and did my best to ignore him.

"None of my business, huh?" She sighs. "The way he stares at you when you're not looking makes me want to fan myself. If a guy looked at me like that, I'd be grinning like the Cheshire Cat."

I yank the dress off the hook. "He's available. Why don't you ask him out?"

A soft snort sounds outside the curtain. "There's an interesting idea."

The dress snags over my raised arms and head. I can't grab it with my hands, so I wiggle and scrunch my shoulders. It doesn't budge an inch. "Damn it!"

"Problem?"

"I'm stuck."

Kelly pokes her head in and chuckles. She steps in and tugs the dress down into place. I stare at the top of her light brown head while she fluffs and smooths the skirt of the dress. She's an attractive woman. Ian would be a fool to turn her down if she asks him out.

My stomach clenches.

If the two of them started dating, then he'd stop asking me out—exactly what I've been telling him I want for a year and a half.

She fastens the dress while I stare into the gold-framed mirror in the corner of the dressing room. It's a beautifully elegant dress with a detailed floral design. Delicate lace accents the top. My brown hair just grazes my jaw line—I'll have to wear it up to stay in style with the dress. I should suggest a floral spray to clip in our hair to Lucinda and Olivia.

Kelly's an inch or two taller than me and gazes over my shoulder at our reflection. They'd be a stunning couple.

I grind my back teeth together and clench my hands into fists.

Why the hell does the image of Ian and Kelly together make me want to punch something?

CHAPTER 2

"*I*'m going to punch you in the face!" Spittle flies from his mouth as he towers over me. He raises his fist in the air. Rage contorts his face. If he follows through, I'm toast. He outweighs me by a solid seventy-five pounds.

I shove back my shoulders and lift my chin. "No you won't. You're going to go to your room and calm down."

"No! I'm going to punch you!" He props his fist on the wall. "I'm going to punch the wall!"

Progress. From bodily harm to property damage. "Remember all the work you had to do to fix the last hole in the wall you made? You had to spend an entire month's allowance on materials. Is it worth it?"

He pulls his arm back and swings at the wall—stopping short of actually punching it.

"Go to your room until you can behave appropriately."

"No! I'm going to run away!"

"Okay, where are you going to go?"

I hold my breath. Nope, not the proper response. The therapist said to concentrate on de-escalating the meltdown. Stay calm. Stress appropriate behavior and consequences.

"I know you're upset. You need to go to your room so you can calm down. You've lost video games for today. If you don't turn this around, you'll lose your phone too. When you can behave respectfully and appropriately, you can come out."

Drew clenches his fists at his sides and stomps his foot. "Move!"

I back several feet out of the way, clearing a path to the hallway and his room. He marches past me and down the hall. The slamming of his door thunders through the apartment.

I fall back against the living room wall and drop my face into my hands. My throat closes as tears fill my eyes. I scrub my hands over my face and sniffle.

Crisis averted. *Get over it.*

I rub my eyes, belatedly remembering I'm wearing makeup, which is probably now smudged all over my face. At least it's the end of the day and not the beginning.

A few more hours and I can crash into bed.

Every time he has a meltdown, I worry the neighbors will hear and call the police. My budget wasn't large enough to afford both a house and the shop. Besides, this apartment over the shop is ideal in every other way. I can work downstairs and still be available for Drew. I own the building, so no added housing expenses. The commute couldn't possibly be better. Then there's the added benefit that from my bedroom window and one of the living room windows, I can see the lake. Pieces of it, anyway, if I peer around or over the buildings across the street.

I push off the wall and glance down the hallway opposite me as I walk over to the kitchen entrance. Silence reigns. There's no smashing or yelling so I take it as a good sign. I peer into the fridge. What will be easy to prepare and is something he won't complain about?

Mac and cheese is his favorite. If I make that, it might help improve his mood. I grab the cheese and milk and then the pasta and flour from the cabinet. It's not only simple, but a comfort food for me too.

When he was younger, his meltdowns could last for hours, not minutes. *Focus on the positives, not the negatives.* At least he's not in his room smashing his belongings or the furniture.

After the pasta is done cooking, I mix it with the cheese sauce I made and pour it into a casserole dish and shove it into the preheated oven.

Drew's bedroom door opens and he shuffles down the hall. I put down the bowls I grabbed to set the table, brace my hands on the counter, and take a few calming breaths. Anger will only aggravate the situation. I need to show him there are other, better, ways to cope with his upsets.

"What's for dinner?"

"Mac and cheese." I turn and wrap my arms around my waist and rest a hip against the counter. "Feel better?"

His belly shows beneath the bottom of his blue T-shirt with the faded car decal across his chest. The shirt is too small. I'll have to find him a new one before he'll allow me to get rid of this one.

He shrugs. "Can I help?"

"You could help set the table by getting the forks and drinks." It's not really a table, but a breakfast bar with an opening between the kitchen and the living room. Since we haven't eaten at the table stuffed into the corner of the living room since we moved in, he knows what I mean.

"Okay."

He grabs two forks from the utensil drawer and then two glasses from the cabinet. I open the fridge to get the water pitcher.

"I got it."

I raise my hands and step back. Drew grabs the water pitcher and swings it so hard water splashes over the top. He brings it over to the bar and pours it into a glass, filling it to the top. He smashes his lips together while he concentrates on pouring water into the second glass. Lights flash in the living room window as a car turns out of the parking lot across the street. Drew looks up and water spills onto the counter.

"Oh shit!" He jumps back, spilling a trail over the bar and counter.

"Language." I'm to blame for his propensity to use that particular curse word. I can hardly punish him when I can't control it coming out of my mouth half the time either. "It's all right. Put the pitcher away and grab a paper towel to clean up the mess."

He jogs over to the fridge, then gets the paper towels. He rips off half the roll and carries the bundle over in his fist. He dabs at the water on the counter and on the floor.

The timer on the oven beeps.

"Go wash your hands and sit."

I wait until we're both sitting and served before turning. "Drew, do you have something to say to me?"

He smiles and shrugs.

"Drew."

"Sorry."

The meltdown is forgotten. It dissipated as quickly as it started. I wish I could get over upsets and forget them as quickly as he does.

I shouldn't have told him they canceled the school fishing field trip so bluntly. I know better. He doesn't tolerate changes to his schedule well. Especially not plans he was looking forward to. That must have been the trigger. His mood had plummeted. He'd become sullen and argumentative over everything. Not that it's out of the norm for him to argue. His oppositional defiant disorder ensures he argues with me over anything from the weather to telling me what I like or dislike.

"Can we watch a show?" Drew shovels a heaping spoonful of mac and cheese into his mouth.

I rub my hand across my aching forehead. "After we finish dinner and clean up the kitchen."

"Okay."

"How was school today?"

He shrugs.

"You know, just because they canceled the school fishing trip, it doesn't mean you can't go fishing. We live across the street from the largest lake in the state. We could rent a boat."

"This weekend?"

"Maybe. I have to check into it, okay?"

He nods and continues eating.

I drink my water and push my bowl away. "I'm going to go change out of my work clothes. You finish eating."

"Can I have the rest of that?" He points to my bowl.

"All yours."

Drew smiles and pulls my bowl next to his.

I place my hand on his shoulder. "Love you."

He shrugs my hand off. "Mm-hmm."

I walk down the hallway to my room across from his and lean back against the closed door with my eyes shut. A painful drumming stabs at my head behind my eyes. I glance at my bed covered in a white puffy comforter in the center of the room. If I lie down now, I won't get back up. Drew will never go to bed on his own. He'll stay up all night until he passes out and be miserable and cranky in the morning when it's time to get up.

After grabbing a set of blue velour lounging clothes from my drawer and putting them on, I walk back down the hall to the bathroom and wash my face. I peek over at the bar, where Drew is still eating. He shovels another forkful of food into his mouth.

Rubbing the soft material of my pants between my fingers, I walk into the kitchen and load the dishwasher. Drew brings over the dishes.

"Go turn on the TV. I'll be there in a minute." It'll take him at least a half hour to choose which show to watch, so it will be bedtime after one episode.

I pop a few pain pills for my headache, put away the leftovers, and wipe down the counters as he flips through the channels. Music, laughter, and cartoon noises all start and stop several times.

I climb into the corner of the couch, tucking my feet underneath me. Another crisis averted. Another day almost done. My bed beckons.

"What's the verdict, kiddo?"

"I'm not a kid."

Technically, seventeen is still a kid, but he likes being considered a man. "No, you're not, but you'll always be my little brother."

"I'm bigger than you."

"Yes, but I'm older."

He nods. "A lot older."

"Watch it buddy." Thirteen years, but it feels more like thirty.

He chortles.

"How about the car cartoon you were watching the other day? Any more episodes of that?"

Drew scrolls through until he locates the show and turns it on. I tilt my head back on the couch and close my eyes. Adrenaline crash or simple exhaustion? Probably a combination. It doesn't matter. I can't go to bed until after he's tucked in and I finish the paperwork for the shop.

He taps me on the head. A bit like I imagine a gorilla would. Whap. Whap. Whap. "Wake up."

I pry open one eye. "I'm not sleeping. I'm resting."

He points to the TV. "Watch."

Drew doesn't like watching shows alone.

I sigh, open my eyes, and prop my head up with my hand. "Okay."

CHAPTER 3

ranny is standing outside the library conference room. I'd recognize that fall of red hair anywhere. Uh oh. Vanessa is standing there too. I quicken my pace. God only knows what sort of trouble that troll is trying to stir up.

"Really, *Fanny*, Mitch is surrounded by the most beautiful women in the world. Don't you think you should put a little more effort into your appearance? But then again, I suppose it's only a matter of time before he comes to his senses."

"Sheath your claws, Vanessa, or I'll do it for you and declaw you like a cat—only a lot more painfully with no anesthesia."

Franny and Vanessa both turn to me.

Vanessa turns red and flounces into the room. I put my arm around Franny's shoulders. "Don't let her get to you."

"I don't. Not anymore." She bumps my arm with her shoulder. "Thanks for the rescue though."

"You know she's only jealous, right?"

"I do, and I'm petty enough to get some satisfaction over the fact it's killing her to know I'm marrying Mitch."

"That's not petty. I would throw it in her face at every opportunity if I were you." If I were marrying a gorgeous celebrity, I'd have T-

16

shirts printed with his face. I'd also make signs and put them up outside her house and place of work. Big ones—billboard size.

Franny chuckles. "How did your fitting go?"

"Perfect. How are the wedding plans going?"

"You'd have to ask Lucinda. She's taken over everything."

"Is that a good thing or a bad thing?"

"Oh, it's a wonderful thing. I'm not into the details like she is, and I know she'll create my vision rather than my mother's."

"Speaking of your mother, she called and ordered a truckload of flower arrangements for your bridal shower."

"Lucinda has promised to keep that in check too. I've never seen her stand up to our mother before, but she goes toe to toe with her over the details. I think she enjoys it."

"Your mother is one of my best customers, as you know, but she is a demanding woman."

"That's a polite understatement." She fiddles with her necklace.

"Why don't we go in and get our seats? Did you bring the goodies?" I look around for the familiar pink box and black writing from Franny's bakery, The Sweet Spot.

"Of course, and I packed a cheesecake bomb for you."

"I love you." I mean those words. Even though I've known her for only about a year, she's my closest friend. One of a chosen few. I used to have dozens of friends blowing up my phone and texting me. That was old Rebecca. New Rebecca's phone rarely makes a peep.

I sigh and scan the room.

The large rectangular room is already full of most of the small business group members. It's going to be a long meeting. The more members that show up, the more questions and comments there are.

"Good evening, people. Why don't we get started?" The members glance over at me. Some smile and wave a greeting while others just grab a seat at the table.

Kelly waves from the end of the table centered in the room and points to the two gray chairs she has saved on either side of her. I nod and grab a cup of coffee and the pink circle of cheesecake coated in a raspberry glaze with a dollop of frosting and a flower on top—pure decadence.

"Before we start, I would like to discuss having a revote for the committee chair. The December vote did not represent the full committee. As you know, I was ill and unable to attend two of the meetings leading up to the vote. Therefore, I wasn't able to properly express my commitment to the voters."

I roll my eyes. It's been four months, and at every meeting, Vanessa makes some sort of dig about my being elected instead of her. This is the first time she's called for a new vote, however.

Franny sits next to Kelly and folds her arms across her waist. "Vanessa, Rebecca won fair and square. Let it go. You're embarrassing yourself."

Vanessa's mouth drops open and then her face scrunches into a scowl.

"Careful, you're going to get wrinkles," I whisper as I walk behind her to my seat on the other side of Kelly.

Vanessa brushes her black hair from her face and lifts her chin. "Does no one agree with me we need a new vote?" She scans the table looking for an accomplice.

When no one agrees, she plops down into her chair with a humph.

Ian strolls in wearing black trousers and a light green button-down shirt with the sleeves rolled back to reveal his tan forearms. The only open chairs are the one to my right and one next to Vanessa. She pulls out the chair and pats the seat.

He glances at the empty chair next to me but slides into the one next to Vanessa.

I haven't seen him since our run-in last week. Maybe I've finally scared him off.

Kelly leans over and whispers in my ear, "You cannot possibly let Vanessa get her hooks into him."

I cross my legs and shrug. "Not my business." If he's dumb enough to hook up with her, he deserves whatever he gets.

Finishing the last morsel of my pink cheesecake bomb, I wipe my mouth and fingers on a napkin and sip my coffee. I clear my throat to get everyone's attention. "It's that time of year, folks. We need to plan the summer festival. Last year was a tremendous success, so let's see if we can top it."

Multiple people talk at once. I stand and hold my hand up until everyone quiets down. Most of my duties as chair are wrangling the lot of the seemingly adult members into taking turns and polite behavior.

"This will go a lot quicker and be more productive if we talk one at a time." I sit, cross my legs, and balance my tablet on my knee. "Okay, Miles, I believe you had something to say. Why don't you start?"

"Fine. I didn't rent a booth last year. I'd like to this year, but as a liquor store owner, it's not like I can hand out samples, so I was wondering what suggestions you might have."

Evie leans forward. "I don't know. Personally, I'd enjoy some of those samples. We should do an adults-only fair some time."

Chuckles fill the room.

"All kidding aside, I don't hand out samples either," Evie continues. "I buy little notepads with my store logo, Pretty Bits, printed on the top and give those out. I figure anytime someone uses the pads, they'll see my logo and think of my souvenir shop."

Derek raises his hand halfway and wiggles his fingers. "I give out coupons with discounts on Petopia services. On the back is a list of my most popular grooming choices."

"I did a raffle last year. People filled out a card with their name and email address and at the end of the fair I drew the winner." Kelly shrugs. "I got a lot of entries, and I think people enjoy the chance to win something. I also added to my contacts list with the emails, so anytime I have a sale, I send a quick newsletter out to the list."

"I, for one, entered that contest. I really wanted the custom-designed dress you gave away." I wink at Kelly.

Kelly smiles. "The winner was a woman from out of town. She needed a dress for her high school reunion. She came back later and told me she reunited with her high school boyfriend at the event. I feel like my dress had a tiny role in a love story."

"Aw, that's really sweet." Franny puts her hand over her chest.

I lean and tilt my head toward her. "Where's Olivia?" She's been a regular at the meetings since she's become a partner at the bakery. She always has great suggestions to share and would be an asset for planning the fair this year.

"Her boys are sick so she couldn't make it today. I promised to take notes." She lifts the notebook. I see a few things scrawled on it. I'll have to call Olivia to check on her and fill her in.

The rest of the meeting is divided between assigning tasks for the festival and discussing events.

I glance up to the clock on the pale yellow wall and close the cover on my tablet. We're already a half hour over, and I need to get home to relieve the babysitter.

"Okay, why don't we table this until next month's meeting? If anyone has anything really pressing, we can email back and forth about it."

The exit shuffle begins. Members gather their belongings and rise from the chairs around the table.

I walk over to the table with the coffee machine and toss my plate and cup into the garbage can underneath.

"Miss me?"

A tingle races down my spine at the deep voice over my shoulder.

"Why on earth would I do that?" I straighten the almost empty bakery box and then move on to the cups.

"Admit it. You'd miss it if I stopped asking you out."

I turn and face him.

His hands are in his pockets and his gaze does a thorough inspection of me. My fingers twitch to smooth my blouse and pants, but I clasp them behind me instead.

"Ian, are you coming? I don't like walking out alone." Vanessa stands behind her chair with her red fingernails drumming on top. She glares at me before smoothing her expression into a simpering smile and bats her eyelashes at Ian.

Ian glances over his shoulder. "Hey, Miles. Walk Vanessa out, will you?"

"Of course." Miles walks over to Vanessa, who frowns at Ian's back before following him out the door.

She's less than subtle with her attempts to grab Ian's interest. She touched his arm twelve times during the meeting, letting her hand linger. Not that I was counting or anything.

Had they ever hooked up?

They're from the same town after all. They both grew up here in Granite Cove.

"Looks like it's just you and me."

I glance up at Ian and then around the room. He's right. Kelly and Franny both abandoned me.

"It's the chase, isn't it? If I said yes, you'd lose interest."

He grins. "Say yes, and let's find out."

"Seriously, you're just not used to women saying no to you—especially after you've already slept with them."

"I can handle rejection just fine."

I plant my fists on my hips. "Really? How many women have told you no? How many have you slept with?"

The corner of his mouth lifts into a smirk. "If you want to know how many women I've slept with, ask."

"I don't give a damn how many women you've had sex with. I'm trying to prove a point." If I am at all curious, it's only in an abstract way. I certainly don't care if he's slept with hundreds. Scratch that. I care. Because ick, that means I'm one of hundreds, making me feel even stupider than I already do for sleeping with him.

"Tell you what. Go out with me, and I'll answer any and all questions you have. We can go get a drink right now."

I walk past him and out of the room, turning the lights off on my way.

"Is that a yes?"

"No, I have plans." Just because they involve paying the babysitter and making sure Drew gets to bed on time doesn't make them any less of a plan.

Ian walks beside me as I march out of the library, shutting off the lights and locking up as I go. He hasn't said a word. Is he giving up?

There's a niggling disappointment I squash like a bug. I do not want to date him or anyone. My life is overflowing with responsibilities, and dating is a responsibility and a stressor. My shop and Drew are all I can handle.

My little red Mustang convertible sits under the parking lot lights waiting for me. It might not be the most practical car and I cringe over the insurance bill, but it's all mine. I splurged on it before my life imploded. It's a reminder of a different life.

The paint gleams under the lights, and I get a puffed-up feeling in my chest. Nope, not going to get rid of my baby. It's one of the few things that still brings me joy.

I expect Ian to branch off and head to his Jeep parked in the next aisle over, but he walks with me to my car. He leans a hand on the side of the door and I scowl at it. I just had the car cleaned, waxed, and detailed.

"Sorry. I forgot how touchy you are about your car. Isn't that usually a guy thing?" He drops his hand with a grin.

"The other day you called me a dog and now a man. Is there really any wonder why I won't go out with you?"

"In my defense, I didn't call you either. I compared certain traits you share."

I open the door and toss my tote onto the passenger seat.

"No one in their right mind could mistake you for a dog or a man."

His gaze travels over me, pausing at my hips and chest, before focusing on my face.

My body floods with warmth. I lick my lips and swallow.

I'm not dead. My body responds to his heated looks.

I throw my shoulders back and raise my chin. I'm stronger than my bodily needs and wants.

"Goodnight, Ian."

He grabs my hand. "One drink." Light as air, his thumb rubs over the pulse in my wrist.

I bite my lip. Temptation washes over me. I could so easily say yes.

But impulsive decisions have landed me in trouble before —with Ian.

"I can't."

He sighs and lifts my hand and kisses my wrist. A shiver of pleasure zings through me.

If I were the same person as I was when I bought my car, I would've said yes. But I'm not that woman anymore.

CHAPTER 4

"*B*lossoms, how can I help you?" Cat twists her blonde ponytail around her finger. "Sure, we can do that." She doodles on the notepad by the phone while she listens. "Tuesday through Saturday, eleven to five. We're closed on Sundays and Mondays. You're welcome."

She hangs up as I lay out a sheet of paper and wrap another flower arrangement to put on display. The readymade bouquets are popular items. People gravitate toward them. Sometimes it's because they know nothing about flowers or don't know how to choose flowers that complement one another. Other times, it's an impulse purchase or a last-minute desperation gift.

"Anything I need to know about?"

"No, a woman wanted to know about funeral flowers and if we make special arrangements. She said she'd stop in sometime this week."

"She didn't want an appointment?"

Cat grimaced. "Should I have told her she needs one?"

"No, it's easier so I can schedule time to work with them, but most people do prefer to walk in. Especially with funerals. There're so many details to take care of, and people are grieving. Flowers are usually at the bottom of the list."

She taps the pen against her chin and frowns. "I've never lost anyone."

"You're young. Count yourself lucky."

Cat still has that special innocence about her that only the young and untouched by tragedy wear. Was I that innocent when I was in college? She's only ten years younger than me, but college seems like another lifetime.

"Have you lost anyone?"

My hands freeze on the baby's breath. A stem snaps off.

"Yes." I drop the broken stem into the trash. "Would you grab some daisies and tulips? I want to make a few more spring bouquets to put on display in the window."

She hesitates but walks over to the wall where all the loose flowers are arranged by type and hanging in rows of silver buckets. I wrap the arrangement in the silver paper and tie it with a baby blue ribbon.

The bell rings over the front door and I glance up.

"Hi, Rebecca."

"Hi, Lucinda. How are you?" It never ceases to amaze me how beautiful she is. I always have the urge to check my appearance and smooth my clothes around her. She epitomizes the term "blonde bombshell." The few pounds she's put on since moving home only enhance her hourglass figure. That she's smart and sweet, too, probably makes her the target of a lot of jealousy.

She walks over like she's sashaying down a catwalk. Her hips sway and the white dress she's wearing swirls at her knees. I've rarely seen her in anything but dresses. Then again, if I had her figure, I'd probably wear them all the time too. She rests her hands on the counter in front of me.

"How much would you hate me if I wanted to make some changes to Franny's flowers?"

"The wedding is still a month away. I won't murder you yet."

She wilts against the counter. "Oh, good!"

Cat carries over the flowers I asked her to get.

"Cat, why don't you put together a bouquet while Lucinda and I discuss her sister's wedding?"

She bites her lip and nods while I walk over to the metal table and baby blue chairs in the corner where I meet with all my appointments. Cat has only worked for me for about six months, but she has a natural talent for flower-arranging. Sometimes she gets a little wild with her color choices, but I have a few customers who love them.

Lucinda pulls out a chair opposite me and sits down while she gazes around the store. "Have I ever told you how much I love how you decorated your shop?"

"You have, but I like to hear it, so say it as often as you like."

She laughs. "Well, I mean it. The blue walls and silver accents throughout are so visually appealing as a backdrop for the colorful flowers. It makes the flowers the focal point, which of course they should be since this is a flower shop."

I want people to recognize the silver paper and blue ribbon as a Blossoms purchase.

"You sure you don't like the blue because it matches your eyes?"

She bats her eyes at me and places her hand under her chin and poses. "You think so?"

I grin and laugh. "Seriously, I chose the silver and blue to offset the colors of the flowers. White might be the obvious choice, but there are several white flowers, so I needed colors not commonly found in plants. Of course, there are blue ones, but baby blue is rarer."

The sign above my store is the same baby blue with silver lettering and a cascade of purple, pink, and white flowers on the side. The tiered display tables sprinkled throughout the store are silver. The potted plants I carry are in baby blue planters with silver lettering.

I unlock the cabinet on the wall behind the table and grab the file for Franny's wedding and open it on the table. The decision to have this built-in cabinet and shelves installed has made my business life so much easier. I no longer need to dash off to my office in back to grab a file for appointments or surprise visits—which often happen.

"What did you have in mind?"

Lucinda opens her white leather hobo purse and pulls out folded pieces of paper from a magazine. She smooths out the pictures of various flower arrangements.

"I don't want to change the bouquets, but I was thinking about the arrangements around the reception and possibly the tables."

"I thought you were going with hurricane lamps on the tables?"

"I was. I am." She shuffles her papers. "What about something like this? A ring of flowers around the lamps. The linens are white, and I think the tables need more color, but I want to keep the elegance of white."

"We could certainly do that."

"But? I can see there's a but."

"Two things." I tap the picture. "I need the dimensions of the lamps, but if I remember correctly, they were fairly large, not small like these. The flower rings are a nice touch. If you really want to add pops of color, I think we could do the flower rings, and how about a small bouquet at each setting as a party favor? Also, these colors are a bit dark for her color scheme."

"Oh, yes. I don't want those heavy colors. How small can you make the bouquets? I don't want people angling their heads around them to hold a conversation. That's the reason we went with the lamps instead of central flower arrangements."

"At some events, it's better to have tall flowers obstructing the view, like when guests don't get along." I wink.

Lucinda laughs and slaps the table. "You do not know how many times I've adjusted the seating charts to accommodate personalities and preferences."

"I bet. We can make them as small as you'd like, but I was thinking…" I hold my hand about four inches off the table. "This way they don't obstruct anyone's vision, including of the flower rings. They'll also be easy for the guests to carry home when the reception is over. I've got some terrific little mirror boxes we can put them in."

"I like that idea. It'll be elegant and pretty, but still casual enough so it's not pretentious."

I jot some notes in the file. "Do you want to specify the flowers in the bouquets or flower rings?"

"I trust you to do whatever you think is best. Have you had your fitting for the bridesmaid dress?"

I nod as I continue with my notes. "You?"

"Unfortunately, yes."

"Problem?"

"I've gained weight. Kelly was really sweet about it and she swears she can make adjustments, but if I gain more, the seams will probably burst and ruin Franny's wedding."

"First, you look fantastic. Second, if your seams do burst, Franny will be happy not to have all the attention on her, as I'm sure every man in the place will have their gazes pinned on you." Franny prefers to blend into the background. Ironic, since she's marrying a celebrity.

She wrinkles her nose. "If men are so interested in me, why can't I get a date?"

"I didn't realize you were looking to start dating."

"My divorce finalized last week."

"Did you celebrate?"

"If eating an entire pint of ice cream can be considered celebrating, then yes." She wrinkles her nose and smiles.

"Sometimes. Did I miss something? Did you change your mind about the divorce?"

She rears her head back. "Of course not!"

"Then why not celebrate? I would have danced in the streets to be rid of that asshole. You should have called me. In fact, why don't we schedule something?"

"You're probably right. I'm glad to be rid of Mark, but the divorce feels like a failure."

"Only for him. You didn't do anything wrong. He's the cheating scumbag. Is he still after you to take him back and have an open marriage?"

"No, he hasn't tried that in a few months."

I reach across and squeeze her hand. "How about I take you to lunch? Cat can watch the shop." I rarely leave for lunch unless I have an appointment I couldn't schedule for Mondays or the time between when Drew goes to school and before the shop opens.

Lunch is all I can offer right now. Nights mean finding a sitter for Drew. Someone who understands how to handle an adult-sized kid with his diagnoses.

"Thanks. I'd like that, but I'm meeting my mother to go over last-minute bridal shower details. Can I have a raincheck?"

"Absolutely. Tell me when and I'll make it happen. Do you need anything for the bridal shower? I feel bad. Here I am, a bridesmaid, but you're handling everything."

She waves a hand. "Planning this wedding has been the highlight of my days lately. You forget, I still don't have a job. Unless you count the times I help Franny out at the bakery."

"Still don't want to get your license to practice law in New Hampshire?"

"No, and it's an argument my mother will be sure to bring up when I see her. She does every single time."

I wince. "You'll find your path. Maybe it's as a wedding planner. Franny raves about everything you're doing every time we talk."

She glances at me and then down to the table and curls the edge of the paper. "I've considered that, actually."

"What's stopping you?"

"A multitude of things. Right now, I have to finish Franny's wedding and then I'll face my future."

A foghorn blares from behind the counter. I leap to my feet.

"What is that noise?"

"My phone." I jog over behind the counter and grab my purse as my heart pounds. Drew's school calling is rarely a good thing.

Cat moves out of my way down the counter.

I dig out my phone and glance at Lucinda. "I'm sorry. I have to take this."

She waves her hand at me, signaling me to go.

I glance between the back door, which leads outside to the parking lot, and the stairs to my apartment. I answer the phone as I push open the door to outside. It's closer.

"Ms. Terrance? This is John Beady, the vice principal at Granite Cove High School. There's been an incident with your brother, Drew."

CHAPTER 5

$\mathcal{T}$he click, click, click of my heels hitting the sidewalk as I jog-walk to the high school entrance echoes in the courtyard. I pull open the gray metal and glass doors, step into the vestibule, and yank on the second set of doors. I stop short of doing a face plant into the door when it doesn't budge, only clicks at me in reprimand when I yank again.

"Can I help you?"

I grimace and turn to the side while pasting a smile on my face. Right, I have to sign in before being allowed into the school. *Way to go, Rebecca.* It's not like it's my first time here, and there are big signs posted all over the place too.

"Sorry, I forgot." I rummage through my purse for my identification. I don't recognize the older woman behind the glass. Someone new, or perhaps she's just filling in today.

"Happens all the time."

"The vice principal is expecting me." I hand over my driver's license and wait while she prints out a sticker with my name and picture.

"You know where you're going?"

NO CHOICE AT ALL

I nod while slapping the sticker on my chest. The door buzzes, and I grab the handle while tossing a "thanks" in her direction.

I dart across the hall to the offices. One of the secretaries looks up as I walk in and gives me an absent smile.

"They're in the conference room." She nods to the hallway on the right.

"Thanks." I stride past the large semi-circular desk taking up half the office space and across to the hallway leading to the individual offices and conference room. She doesn't bother asking if I know the way. I've been here many times before.

The blinds are open on the glass walls so I can see Drew sitting at the conference table with the vice principal at the head of the table and a brunette across from my brother with her back to me. When I open the door, all eyes focus on me.

Familiar hazel eyes blink at me. She glances between Drew and me, probably trying to guess the connection. Kerry Barton. Why is she in here with Drew? I know she's a teacher here, but since when is she one of his?

Great, now I'll have more questions to answer. We belong to the same book club and are friendly, but not enough to share the details of my private life.

Mr. Beady nods at me as I pull out the chair next to Drew. "Ms. Terrance, thank you for coming in."

"Of course." I set my purse on the empty chair next to me and smile at Drew. "Hey, buddy. How are you doing?"

Drew shrugs and gives me a small smile.

"Do you know Ms. Barton? She's a teacher here. The incident occurred outside her classroom."

"Yes, Kerry and I are in a book club together."

She leans forward and smiles. "I didn't realize Drew was your brother. I see the resemblance though."

I glance at him. We do share the same shade of brown hair and the same full lips and heart-shaped face, but he's got Mom's light brown eyes and Dad's tall, muscular frame. My eyes are dark brown—or "witchy black," as an ex-boyfriend described them. Of course, he also told me I have a witch's black heart when I dumped him. Maybe he just had a fixation with witches.

Drew's knee is bouncing, and he's picking at a scab on his arm. I reach for my purse to grab a pack of tissues but spot the box on the table and pluck one out and hand it to him. He'll pick until it bleeds. There's no point in trying to get him to stop right now. Half the time he doesn't even realize he's doing it. It's compulsory and why I always have to carry a supply of bandages.

"As I told you on the phone, Drew kicked another student's backpack. He knocked it off the student's arm and then kicked it again when it fell on the floor."

I look from Mr. Beady to Kerry. "You witnessed this?"

"I only saw him kick it once it was on the floor. I heard a commotion outside my room and went to investigate. When I asked the students what happened, they said Drew had kicked the backpack from the boy's arm. Drew wouldn't answer any of my questions." She smiles at Drew. "Are you ready to tell us what happened, Drew?"

He shrugs and stares up at the ceiling.

"None of the students could provide a reason for his behavior."

"Who was this boy?"

Mr. Beady frowns. "We can't divulge the student's identity."

Of course, I should have known that. I sigh. "Okay, is there any history with this student and my brother?"

"None that we are aware of."

"Did anyone witness the whole incident? An adult? Where was his para?"

"She was with another student."

I clench my hands together in my lap. "According to his IEP he's supposed to have a paraprofessional throughout the day."

Mr. Beady straightens in his chair. "He had a para in class. She was working with him and another student."

"He's also supposed to have one during transition from one class to another." In order to avoid situations just like this from happening. Drew's go-to method is to shut down instead of speaking up for himself. Although he is certainly capable of kicking someone's backpack, there had to be some reason.

"Ms. Terrance, there was a hall monitor."

"Did this hall monitor witness the incident?"

His gaze drops to the table. "No. However, there is no dispute that Drew did kick the backpack. Ms. Barton did witness the second kick."

Drew's head rotates from side to side and back and forth—over and over.

I compress my lips. He is done. The stimming behavior will likely increase and he'll become agitated if I don't get him out of here.

"Look, I understand if Drew did in fact kick the backpack there needs to be consequences. My point is if no one actually witnessed the entire incident then we can't be sure what happened." I glance at Kerry. "Is it possible the backpack fell in front of him and he used his foot to push it out of the way to avoid tripping over it?"

She opens her mouth and then closes it again. "I suppose it is possible if you disregard what the other students said."

I turn my head back to Mr. Beady. "This is why a para needs to be with him at all times. He can't advocate for himself—yet." I glance at Drew. He rocks back and forth in the chair. "He's had enough." I stand and grab my purse. "Will a note of apology to this unidentified student be sufficient or do you intend to punish my brother further?"

Yeah, maybe I was being a bitch, but what the hell was the point of having an IEP to list all his unique requirements and accommodations if they weren't going to follow it?

"I think that will suffice. I'll ensure he has a paraprofessional with him throughout the day going forward as stated in his individualized education plan."

"Thank you." I glance down at Drew. "Come on, buddy. Time to go home." I touch him lightly on the shoulder. He pulls away and stands.

"I'll let everyone know Drew is going home for the day." Mr. Beady taps away on his laptop.

Kerry stands. "Goodbye, Drew. I'll see you tomorrow."

He doesn't respond as we walk out of the room. I wave. This will probably make interactions at future book club meetings awkward. I know I put her on the spot in there, but I can't worry about possible hurt feelings. Drew is my priority. I'm all he's got. If I don't stand up for him, no one else will.

She walks alongside me down the hall. "Drew is always smiling when I see him… Well, except for today."

I peek to the side at her profile. She's frowning and chewing on her lip.

A hard finger poke jabs into the back of my shoulder—repeatedly.

I wince and hunch my shoulders forward. "Drew, stop pushing me."

His finger poke signals anything from "I want your attention or affection" to "Get me the hell out of here."

Kerry glances over her shoulder at Drew and smiles. I sense her gaze on me as we enter the central office area. I'm sure she has many questions, but now is not the time to answer any of them.

"Bye, Kerry. Drew, say goodbye to Ms. Barton."

"Bye." His deep voice rumbles behind me as I open the door. He looks and sounds like a man, but he only just turned seventeen, and his maturity level is significantly lower. People don't know that by looking at him though.

He's quiet while I sign out and we walk out to the car. After a few moments, a slight smile appears on his face and he leans forward to play with the radio. He loves riding in my car. Another reason I won't trade it in for a more reasonable sedan or practical SUV.

Snippets of songs change in rapid succession. When was the last time I heard an entire song with Drew in the car?

"You want to tell me what happened today?"

"I don't know." He shrugs and continues playing with the radio.

"Did you kick the boy's backpack on purpose?"

Another shrug.

"What's his name?"

Silence. I glance over at him. I can tell by his blank stare he's trying to access the information in his brain. It's in there somewhere. It just takes him a bit longer than others to process it.

Another couple of minutes pass. "Drew? Do you know his name?"

"Josh?"

A question at the end. So, either he's not sure of the name or he's not feeling confident about the conversation.

"Is Josh nice to you?"

He drops his hand from the radio, shrugs, and looks out the window.

Should I push for answers? It's always a fine line between getting information and agitating him too much so he shuts down.

"Broke my pencil."

My fingers grip the steering wheel. "Josh broke your pencil?"

"Yeah, my Mustang pencil."

I clench my teeth together so I don't let out the string of curse words screaming in my mind. Drew's favorite pencil, which he refuses to sharpen because he doesn't want it to get used up. I've searched for other pencils, but I've only found generic vehicle pencils. None with only Mustangs on it. I found it in a rest stop on our last visit to New York. I don't exactly relish driving six hours to replace a pencil.

"Was it an accident?" Josh could have broken it by mistake and Drew got upset.

"He took it from me and went like this." He holds his hands up next to each other and mimics snapping the pencil in half.

Son of a bitch!

I glance at the clock on my dashboard. We'll be home in five minutes. Another five to ten minutes to get Drew situated and check in with Cat to make sure she's handling the store on her own okay, and then Mr. Beady is going to get a phone call from me about a bully named Josh.

"Called me dumb."

I grind my teeth so hard my jaw aches. Tears fill my eyes but I blink them back as I turn into the parking lot behind my building.

That little pissant is going to wish he'd never been born by the time I get done with him.

My blood pressure is skyrocketing like one of those strength test carnival games.

I swerve into an open parking space and hit the brakes hard

enough to lock the seatbelts. I throw the car into park and turn off the engine. I lift my hand to touch his arm, then drop it onto my lap and take several deep breaths until I trust myself to speak coherently.

As much as I'd like to confront the bully myself, I'd be the one to get in trouble. Adults can't go around beating up kids or even lecturing them heatedly on proper behavior. But, boy, that would be satisfying. I guarantee he'd never bother my little brother again.

"Drew, honey, he had no right to treat you that way. He's a bully, and bullying is wrong. Why didn't you tell anyone what he did?"

He shrugs and continues looking out the window. "Can we go in?"

I rub the spot between my eyebrows. "Just a second. I know it's hard to find the words sometimes, but it's important. Instead of kicking his backpack and getting in trouble, you should have told a teacher what he did so he was the one who got in trouble. Understand?"

And like hell is Drew going to write a note of apology to that little shit.

"Can we go in now?"

"Do you understand?"

He nods.

"Okay, let's go."

He jogs over to the back stairs to the apartment and takes them two at a time while I grab my purse out of the backseat and lock the car. He's already punched in the code on the door and disappeared inside by the time I reach the stairs.

The incident is all but forgotten for him until he goes to look for his favorite pencil again.

Kids can be so damn cruel.

CHAPTER 6

The store door chimes, signaling a customer, while I wash my hands in the bathroom at the back of the store. One of the many reasons I wish I could afford to hire an extra assistant so there's always someone else working with me. I snatch a paper towel from the dispenser and dry my hands while I stride to the front, bemoaning the fact I can't afford to hire another part-timer to help with the store.

Ian stands in the center of the store with his hands on his hips. His well-worn jeans and white polo shirt show off his fit body to mouth-watering perfection. There's a hitch in my chest that makes me want to smash something. Why the hell am I attracted to the wrong men? It's like some cosmic joke with the powers that be lounging around deciding which mismatched individuals they can throw together so they can be entertained by the chaos that ensues.

"Afternoon."

"What can I do for you?" I toss the paper towel into the garbage can under the counter, spread my palms on the surface, and raise my chin to meet his gaze. I am a professional store owner, and he will not get a rise out of me today.

He strolls over and leans with his elbow resting on top of the counter. I resist the urge to peek over to see how he's accomplishing the pose without looking ridiculous since he's tall and the counter is waist high on me. Instead, I step back and clasp my hands behind me.

"I need a couple of bouquets."

A couple? It's not like I'm surprised he's juggling women. In fact, I'm sure he's dating several. I hold no illusions he's pining away for me.

"All right. Do you have any specific flowers you'd like to use? And are the bouquets going to be the same or different?"

"Different. I wouldn't want to appear unoriginal. Make sure they're both equally nice though. I don't want to look like I'm playing favorites."

"They know about each other enough to compare? What, are you dating roommates or something?"

He smirks and turns to rest both arms on the counter in front of me. "Jealous?"

Why didn't I keep my mouth shut? I roll my eyes. "Hardly." I walk over to the wrapping area and unroll two strips of paper and lay them on the counter. "What about colors? Any preferences? Price point?"

Not going to comment on anything personal. Who he dates or how many is none of my business.

"Let's see, make one with pastel colors. She prefers softer shades. And the other with some red. She goes for more bold colors, and red is her favorite."

"Okay."

He knows what colors they each like. I'd be mildly impressed if I didn't think it was part of his act to trick a woman into feeling like she's special.

I pluck out an assortment of pink tulips and roses, lavender, and white carnations from the coolers and blue buckets on the shelves. I carry them back to the counter and add some greenery before making the first bouquet.

"Suitable?"

"Very pretty. You go to school for that?" He tilts his head. "Do they have florist school?"

"They do and no, I didn't. I worked for a florist throughout college." I took a couple of courses in floral arrangement and botany while earning my business degree, but he doesn't need to know that.

I pick a half dozen red roses for the next bouquet and reach for the baby's breath.

"How about those tall ones?"

His warm breath fans the back of my neck and I freeze. He followed me over here. His arm brushes mine as he points to the gladiolus. A shiver dances down my spine.

"They'll be more expensive since they aren't in season."

"That's fine. She likes those."

I switch out the red roses for white and add the red gladiolus. He knows the flowers they like too—well, one of them anyway.

After I wrap the second bouquet, I raise an eyebrow and stare at him. "Anything else?"

He winks. "Nope, the moms should be happy with these."

"The moms? These are for your mother?"

"Mothers. I have more than one."

"Oh." His parents must have divorced and his father remarried. Fairly common in this day and age. Probably more likely than parents staying together.

"My mom and dad divorced when I was a teenager, and five years ago today, she married Susan. The flowers are for their anniversary."

"Ah, I get it. Do you really call them 'the moms'?"

"Only when I'm talking to someone else. Otherwise they're Mom and Susan. Dad remarried, too, so I've got another stepmother besides Susan, Rose."

"So, three mothers."

"Yup. I'd say family get togethers are interesting, but they all get along really well."

"That's fortunate."

"You could see for yourself. There's a family picnic today to celebrate the anniversary. Come with me. I'll pick you up after work."

I open my mouth to refuse when the door chimes and Franny and Lucinda walk in. Franny's eyes widen when she spots Ian.

"Did we have an appointment?" I never forget appointments.

"No, we came to say hello and see if you are available for a girls' night."

Ian smiles and nods in their direction. "Ladies."

"Hello, Ian. Have you met my sister, Lucinda?" Franny waves a hand toward her as they approach the counter.

"I don't believe I've had the pleasure."

He gives her that half-smile half-smirk he probably thinks is sexy and charming. Like he's saying "I know exactly how to pleasure you."

All right, it might be a tad sexy.

"You graduated a few years ahead of me, but I remember watching you and your brothers play basketball. You had all the girls' hearts aflutter."

Ian chuckles. "Including yours?"

My gaze darts between them. The two of them are both gorgeous and flirting masters. I'm surprised they haven't run into each other before and started dating. I suppose it's inevitable.

"Of course." Lucinda plants a hand on her hip and gives him a sultry grin.

A crash booms from upstairs.

Everyone's gaze rises to the ceiling while mine darts to the camera monitor under the counter.

Drew's room is empty.

"Excuse me." I run down the hallway and up the stairs tucked into the back corner of the building. The door at the top is still wide open like I left it this morning when I came downstairs to the store.

"Drew?"

I look across the entryway into the kitchen. There's broken glass and globs of something on the floor.

I sprint over to the kitchen opening. Drew is standing on the other side of the mess.

"I was making pudding."

"Okay, honey, don't move. I don't want you to cut your bare feet on the glass."

"Okay."

There's someone's tread on the interior stairs. I look behind me. Ian, followed by Franny and Lucinda, come up the stairs.

Shit!

"Who's that?" Drew steps forward to see.

"No! Watch out."

He stops with a foot in the air and stares at the floor. "Oh, yeah. I forgot."

"Everything okay?"

I wince and glance over my shoulder. Ian stands in the opening, staring at Drew. Franny and Lucinda peek around him.

Great. Just what I need. Now I'll have to make explanations.

"Everything's fine. I'll be back down in a few minutes."

Nobody moves.

I sigh and turn fully around. *So be it.* "This is my brother, Drew. Drew, this is Ian and my friends Franny and Lucinda."

Drew waves enthusiastically and grins. I smile at his eagerness. Franny and Lucinda are my friends. There's no reason they can't meet my brother.

Franny and Lucinda both wave back. Ian smiles and steps into the kitchen. They follow close behind him, glancing between Drew and me.

I grab the dustpan from under the sink.

"Here, I'll get that while you work on the wet stuff." Ian grabs one side of the dustpan.

I hold on to my side. "Thanks, but I've got it."

He tugs it out of my hands and crouches down to the floor.

Franny walks in and grabs the roll of paper towels from the holder under the upper cabinet. She tears a bunch off and hands them to Lucinda as they both squat and start cleaning up the mess. I stare at the tops of their heads for a few seconds before pulling the garbage can out and grabbing the cleaner and wipes.

We clean the mess up within minutes with the four of us working together.

"Sissy, can I move now?"

"Oh, honey, I'm sorry. Yes, but go this way." I direct him to the edge of the kitchen. "There could still be some fragments of glass. Go put some socks on."

Ian wipes a wet paper towel over the area again. "I think it's safe."

"Thank you, all of you, for your help."

Franny looks down the hallway where Drew disappeared. "Is he visiting you?"

"No, Drew lives with me. I'm his guardian."

She frowns, and I know she's wondering why she's never met Drew before now and why I haven't mentioned him.

It's not like it's a secret. I simply don't volunteer my life history to everyone I meet.

Drew comes back down the hallway wearing his favorite rainbow-colored striped socks. He's smiling from ear to ear. He loves people. It didn't used to be that way. He used to have selective mutism and would shut down and hide behind me in social situations. Now, he gets excited meeting people and talking to them.

I guess my old habits of not inviting people to our home needs to end.

"Look, Sissy bought me new socks." He lifts his feet one at a time to show everyone.

Lucinda grins. "I like them. I should get a pair like that. They look comfy."

"She means it too. My sister has a drawer full of what she calls comfy socks."

"And what's wrong with that?" Lucinda frowns at Franny.

"Nothing, except you might be developing a fetish because the last few times we've gone to the store together you've bought new pairs. How many socks does one person need?"

"They're warm and my feet get cold."

"I like socks too. And cars." Drew grins.

Lucinda steps next to him and nods. "I'm with you, Drew."

"Do you want to see my room?"

"I'd love to." Lucinda follows him down the hallway.

Franny chuckles. "Luce has made another conquest."

I glance at Ian leaning against my kitchen counter with his arms folded over his chest and his ankles crossed.

"Let's go downstairs so I can ring up your flowers."

"I'm not in a hurry."

I frown at him but he doesn't move.

"So, are you free for that girls' night or do you have other plans?" Franny looks at Ian and back to me.

"I'm sorry, I can't. There's no one to watch Drew tonight."

"You could bring him to my moms' picnic. Boys are allowed there."

I stare at him. The man doesn't give up.

The store's front door chimes. I grimace and stride for the stairs. "I need to get downstairs."

"I'll stay here with Lucinda and Drew, if it's okay with you."

I glance over my shoulder at Franny and nod. "Thanks." I glare at Ian. "Coming?"

He pushes off the counter and follows me down the stairs.

Ian waits, leaning on the counter, while I help the customer pick out one of the premade bouquets. The back of my neck tingles from his watching gaze the entire time.

As soon as the door closes, I swivel and ring up his bouquets. He pays me without a word. He puts his wallet away and picks up the flowers. I almost sigh in relief. No questions. No more innuendo.

"Pick the two of you up at five or do you need some time after closing?"

"I'm not going to your mothers' party." It was sweet the way he helped clean up, but it's not enough to get me to cave on my no-dating rule.

"Just Drew then? No problem. I'm sure I'll learn a lot about you from him."

"Very funny. Neither of us are going." I fold my arms over my waist. "Thanks for the invitation."

The corner of his mouth kicks up in a smile. "Sure thing, Buttercup."

I roll my eyes. "Another ridiculous nickname?"

"Have to keep trying until I find one that works." He winks and strolls out the door.

CHAPTER 7

"*R*eady to go?"

I pinch the bridge of my nose and squeeze my eyes shut. If I ignore him, will he go away?

Of course, he won't. Ian's middle name is persistence. I know I was very clear when I told him I wasn't going to his mothers' anniversary party. Yet here he is, waltzing in my door five minutes before closing.

I open my eyes and glare at him. I was watching the clock tick down to closing so I could go upstairs and change into comfy clothes and drink an enormous glass of wine—or two. Franny and Lucinda left about an hour ago after spending the afternoon with Drew and me in the store. They played cars with him on the table, using various paraphernalia around my shop to create roads and buildings for his cars. Drew was ecstatic.

Franny said she understood when I explained I hadn't deliberately kept him a secret from her, but that it had become an ingrained habit to protect him and avoid complicated explanations.

Her words conveyed understanding, but her face said something else entirely. She was hurt I hadn't shared something so important to me with her.

How was I going to fix this?

NO CHOICE AT ALL

That's what I need to focus on, not Ian and his refusal to accept no.

The bathroom door squeaks as Drew walks out.

Crap! I forgot he was in there.

"Hey, Drew. Ready to go to my family picnic?"

My mouth drops open. He did not just say that to my brother.

Drew grins. "Picnic?"

"Yeah, it'll be a blast. Tons of food. Games. Hey, you like animals? My mom lives on a farm."

"Animals? What kind?"

How bad would it be if I launch myself across the counter and strangle Ian to death?

"Horses, goats, chickens, dogs, cats."

It would be bad. I'd go to jail, and there would be no one to take care of Drew.

"Sissy? Are we going?"

I peek up at him standing next to me. His eyes are wide and his mouth is slightly open like he can't believe this is happening.

If there's one thing Drew loves as much, if not more, as cars, it's animals.

He had a dog, but she passed away before we moved here. I've been so busy establishing my business and getting us both settled that I've been putting off his pleading for a new pet. The thought of taking on the added time and stress of a puppy makes me want to curl up in a ball and hibernate like a bear.

"Did I mention some of those cats are actually kittens?"

I send a death glare at Ian as Drew sucks in an audible breath of excitement.

"Honey, pick up your cars and take them upstairs." I nod over to the table. He gets a worried look on his face and turns his gaze to Ian.

There's no way I can disappoint him.

"After you do, you can get your shoes and sweatshirt on."

His face lights up and he runs over to the table. The metal cars ping against one another as he tosses them one by one into the plastic container he carried them down in.

"Do you..."

I snap up a finger in Ian's face as soon as he opens his mouth and shake my head. If he says one word before Drew goes upstairs, I may give in to my murderous tendencies.

A wave of heat rolls over my tightened skin. My hand trembles. I lower it to my side and clench my fingers into a fist.

Wisely, he says nothing more while Drew finishes loading his cars into the container. I walk over and lock the front door and switch the sign to closed.

"What do I do now?"

"Put them away in your room and get your shoes and sweatshirt on."

He nods and jogs down the hall and up the interior stairs. His heavy tread echoes through the building. He would never make it as a ninja. Quiet he is not.

I swivel on my toes to face Ian.

"How dare you use my brother to get me to go out with you!" I poke him in the chest. "That's low, even for you."

He raises both hands in the air. "Easy, killer. What's the harm of going to a family picnic? He'll have fun. And so will you if you relax."

"Don't tell me to relax! And that is not the point!"

I step forward, inches from his chest, and glare up at him. "What makes you think I want to go back for seconds? If the first—and only —time had been so great, don't you think I would've said yes to one of your dozens of invitations?"

He gazes down at me and then leans his face a breath away from mine. "What are you so afraid of, killer? You've been running scared. That tells me it meant something, otherwise you'd be indifferent. And that is one thing you're not, baby."

I suck in a breath, ready to blast him with my rage.

His gaze drops to my mouth. "You're right." He steps back and stuffs his hands in his pockets.

I blink, and my chest deflates. *Excuse me?*

"I'm sorry. I shouldn't have involved your brother."

"No, you shouldn't have." Well, that was a surprise.

"I can't find my sweatshirt!" Drew's bellow down the stairs makes me wince. At least there are no customers.

I forgo the usual statement—if he would hang it on the hook in the closet, he would know where it was—and walk closer to the stairs so I don't have to yell. "Check the couch." He'd worn it to school yesterday, and I remember him yanking it off while he was watching TV.

His stomps drift down the stairs. I can track the sounds of his movement across the apartment.

"Found it!"

"You still going?" Ian's voice sounds behind me.

I glance over my shoulder to find him standing close. I step back and wrap my arms around my waist.

"Only because I don't want to disappoint Drew." I look down at my skirt and blouse. "I need a few minutes to change. You might as well go up to the apartment so I can lock up the shop." He walks to the foot of the stairs. "To be clear, I am not running scared from you or anything else."

Ian doesn't comment. He turns and climbs the stairs.

After I cash out the register, lock everything up, and set the alarm, I walk up the stairs to find Ian and Drew sitting on the floor in the living room playing cars. They're using the designs on the area rug as their road map.

My heart gives a little jump. Drew doesn't really have any men in his life, other than a couple of teachers at school. It's not nearly the same thing. How am I supposed to fix that?

I can't date a man just to give Drew male role models. There're way too many possible complications that could arise—for him and for me.

"I'll be ready in a few minutes."

Other than a quick glance from Ian, they ignore me.

I go into my bedroom and pull on a pair of black jeans, a maroon T-shirt, and sneakers. I'll pretend this picnic is networking in the community for potential customers. Once we're there, I'm sure Ian will have plenty of family members wanting his attention. Drew and I can slip away and visit with the animals. After an appropriate amount of time, I'll call a car service to pick us up.

Running scared?

As if! I might not be indifferent to him, but that doesn't mean I'm running scared. That's his ego talking. He simply can't comprehend a woman isn't interested in going out with him.

I snatch a black hoodie from my closet and yank it on.

It's ridiculous. I'm not scared of anything, least of all him. I've survived the worst life could throw at me.

He's nothing to me, and it's about damn time he accepts that.

CHAPTER 8

"*D*o you know that cat has only ever let one person get anywhere near him?"

The only cat I see is the gray-and-white one with double paws curled up and drooling in Drew's lap. He spent a fair amount of time with the kittens when we arrived, but the mama kitty got agitated, so I convinced Drew to check out the rest of the farm.

I raise an eyebrow and glance up over my shoulder at the woman leaning against the railing above the one I parked my butt against. Her salt and pepper gray hair falls in a straight line to below her chin. Turquoise blue glasses hide her eyes behind tinted lenses. A relative of Ian's? Friend of the family?

Drew had plopped down on the ground outside the barn as soon as the cat waltzed out and twined between his legs. I'd winced at the possibilities he was sitting on, but only sighed and gone over to the paddock attached to the barn.

"Yes, that one currently in a love affair."

I chuckle. "Drew has a way with animals." I raise a hand up to her. "I'm Rebecca, and that's my brother, Drew."

"Molly, Ian's mother."

"Oh." I stand and dust off the back of my pants. When we arrived,

I'd instructed Ian to go away and he'd listened. I was still angry with him over manipulating me into coming by using my brother. Drew had made a beeline for the barn and I'd followed. I hadn't spoken to anyone at the party.

I glance at the woman who's probably wondering who the hell I am and why I arrived with her son but haven't spoken to him since.

She tilts her head in my direction. "You came with Ian."

"Yes, we did. I own the flower shop in town, Blossoms. He invited us after purchasing bouquets for your anniversary. Congratulations."

"Thank you, and the flowers are beautiful." She continues gazing at me expectantly.

I stuff my hands into the front pocket of my hoodie. "We're... acquaintances from the town small business group. I hope you don't mind he invited us."

"Why would I?"

"Well, we're strangers, and this is a family picnic."

"Friends often become family, and we have plenty of food to share."

"Thank you."

"You're new to town, aren't you?"

"I bought the shop almost two years ago. We've lived here about a year and a half."

"And where are you from originally?"

"New York. Upstate." A strand of hair blows across my cheek. I tuck it behind my ear and fold my arms across my waist.

"Do you still have family there?"

My thumb presses against the birthstones of my mother's ring.

"My cousin."

She rests a hand on my shoulder. "It must be difficult raising your brother on your own."

I blink at her. How does she know I'm raising Drew? Did Ian say something to her? What had he said? What does he know?

"I... It..." I let out a whoosh of breath. "Yes."

She slips her arm around my waist and gives me a squeeze. Tears prick my eyes.

Jesus, what is this woman doing to me? I'm practically ready to start bawling. Over what?

"Steve, Ian's father, and I divorced when the boys were all teenagers." She points to a tall man standing in front of a picnic table full of people. "I suddenly became a single mom. Don't get me wrong. Steve is, and always has been, a wonderful father—very involved. But that feeling of me against the world brought me to my knees more than once. It can be overwhelming."

I swallow hard and run my tongue over my teeth. I've been on my knees and curled into a ball of abject misery at a complete loss of how to go on more times than I can count.

"Then I met Susan."

She nods toward a woman with a big bawdy laugh over by the grill. She must be at least six feet tall with a thick braid of gray and black hair hanging down her back.

I smile. "Was it love at first sight?"

"I believe it was. She just lit up the room with her personality. I was immediately drawn to her." She glances away from Susan and looks at me. "I love the person, not the gender."

"That's a beautiful sentiment. I've never heard it described so eloquently and succinctly before."

A pair of goats' broken *baas* call from a pen next to the paddock behind us. The creatures dance around, nudging each other out of the way at the gate.

Molly laughs. "They want attention."

A teenage girl runs over and feeds them something from her hand.

"That's Katy, the daughter of a friend of Rose's, Steve's wife."

"Ian mentioned you all get along really well."

She chuckles and nods. "We do. Steve and Rose are my closest friends. We even go on vacation together."

"I imagine that's rather rare."

"I hope not, because it's a wonderful support system to have, especially when kids are involved."

"It sounds wonderful."

"Who's your support system, Rebecca?"

I blow out a breath and look up at the blue sky and puffy white clouds drifting by overhead. How do I answer that question? Me, myself, and I?

Drew pulls a couple cars out of his pocket carefully, so as not to disturb the sleeping cat, and plays with them in the dirt.

"I was twenty-two when our parents died. I've been his guardian for eight years. I was thirteen when he was born."

She gives me a side squeeze with the arm still wrapped around my waist. Why haven't I stepped away? Why do I find her embrace comforting and maternal instead of invasive? I'm not one to enjoy casual affection. I'm not a hugger or toucher. I guess Drew and I have that in common.

I glance at her out of the corner of my eye. If any other stranger had walked up to me and put their arm around me, I would have politely but firmly stepped away and put distance between us. If they had asked deeply personal questions, I would have changed the subject. If they persisted, I would have walked away.

She sniffles, and my gaze shoots up to her face. There are tears tracking down her cheeks.

Surely not over me? I look out over the partygoers for the source of her upset. Or are those happy tears for watching her family celebrate her anniversary?

"You must be a very brave woman."

"Brave, how?"

She tilts her head up. "To take on the responsibility of raising your brother amid your grief."

"I wasn't brave. I was terrified." Still am a lot of the time.

"That's the definition of brave, dear. Doing something despite the fear."

I scrunch my shoulders. "It's not like it was a choice. There was no one else."

"There's always a choice. You made the decision to raise him."

I grimace and shake my head. "He's my brother. I couldn't let him go into foster care or anything."

"Some would."

Yeah, some would, and some tried to convince me to do the same.

A black and white chicken wanders out of the barn and pecks at the ground. Drew waggles his fingers toward it, but it ignores him and waddles past.

She rubs my back before dropping her arm, then takes a few steps closer to Drew. "The two of you must be hungry. Why don't we join the party?"

Drew lifts his head at the mention of food.

"Hungry?"

He grins.

"He's the perpetual bottomless pit."

"All teenage boys are."

"What about the cat?" Drew frowns down at the cat in his lap.

Molly chuckles and walks over to him. The cat opens one eye and looks at her, then leaps off his lap and hightails it into the barn.

"Sarge only tolerates one other person besides you, and that's Ian." She grins down at Drew while he stares at where the cat disappeared.

"Why do you call him Sarge?" Drew squints up at her.

"Because he reminded me of a grumpy old soldier when he showed up one day. He was injured, had a limp. I tried for hours to lure him out so I could take him to the vet. Finally, Ian showed up. The cat hopped out of hiding and gazed up at my son with a pitiful look. Ian scooped him up and took him to the vet. Now every time he needs a checkup, I call Ian."

Drew stuffs his cars back into his pocket and stands. He yanks on the elastic waistband of his athletic pants, which tend to drift low whenever he sits. I wish I could find a pair of jeans with a special fastener he could manage.

Molly tucks her arm through Drew's. He doesn't flinch or pull away. He even bends his arm slightly to accommodate hers. What is this woman's superpower?

"I'll show you where you can wash your hands and then we'll fill that empty belly of yours."

They stroll off toward the house.

Once I manage to close my mouth, I follow them.

The white farmhouse is about twenty feet away from the barn. Giant half barrels filled with red geraniums flank the concrete back steps. Drew holds the door for her and they walk inside without even looking to see if I'm coming with them. Another first.

"Hey."

I glance to the side at Ian standing next to me, staring at the house Drew just disappeared into.

"Your mother is an amazing woman."

He looks down at me and searches my face for I don't know what. "She is."

"You have competition for Sarge's affections."

"Is that so?"

"Yes, he was curled up, drooling in Drew's lap."

He chuckles. "That cat is particular."

"So Molly said."

"Looks like I need to buy my mother more flowers."

I frown and peer up at him. "Why is that? Did something happen to the bouquet?"

"No, but somehow she got you to stop looking like you wanted to murder me and join the party."

My cheeks heat and I glance away.

CHAPTER 9

The bus pulls away, and I wave even though I can't see Drew through the darkened windows. After the incident with the backpack last week, I get a knot in my stomach every day he goes to school. The principal, vice principal, and the special education director have all assured me a para will be with Drew at all times. And Drew has been happy, and he says everything is good every time I ask. I have to have some faith in the system, right? What's the alternative?

Sighing, I turn and stride down the sidewalk to the alleyway between my building and the new candy store, Sugar Rush, that opened this past year. The owners haven't been to a small business group meeting yet. I should stop in and give them the spiel. Vanessa said she had done it when they first opened, but it doesn't hurt to try again. Small businesses in town need to band together. We're stronger as a group.

A cold drop of rain hits the tip of my nose—at least I hope it's rain. I glance up at the mixture of gray and white clouds hanging over the town as I swipe a finger over my nose and make sure it is water and not bird poop. Clear. My lips twitch into a smile as I flip the hood of my navy blue jacket up over my head.

Dark splats hit the sidewalk, turning the concrete into a path of polka dots of light and dark gray. I quicken my pace in case the weather report was wrong and the sprinkles turn into a deluge. Franny's bakery is only a few blocks down and across the street. I won't get soaked—hopefully.

Instead of entering the bakery's front where I can see a handful of customers milling about and Olivia and Sally running the register, I walk down the alleyway between The Sweet Spot and Skis 'n' Things.

Franny's hurt expression from Saturday has been gnawing at me for days. She's one of my few actual friends here in Granite Cove. I need to make this right. I picked up the phone to call her a few times, but this needs to be a face-to-face conversation. Her shop is closed Mondays and Tuesdays, and I didn't want to encroach on her time with Mitch since I know he just got back into town after spending the past two weeks in Los Angeles for work. He's got some big directing job filming in Boston coming up this summer.

A chilly breeze blowing off the lake hits me as I round the back corner of the building. I hunch my shoulders a bit as goosebumps break out over my arms. The lake is alive with rolling waves splashing against the seawall. Hard to believe only last month ice still coated the water's surface.

A frigid gust of wind blows my hood down and blasts the back of my neck as I knock on the back door of the bakery and peer into the kitchen, hoping to get a glimpse of Franny. I probably should have called first. I've never appeared at her kitchen door before.

The sun reflecting off the windows makes it hard to see inside, but I see a human-shaped shadow moving toward me before the door opens.

"Rebecca?"

I wave at Franny, who's staring at me with a puzzled expression on her face. I shake my head slightly. She's not wearing a speck of makeup, but her ivory skin is flawless. I've heard her complain about her orange hair more than once, but a lot of women would, and do, pay to have her natural color. She's got it twisted up in a bun on top of her head. She and Lucinda don't look much alike at first glance, but they have the same classically beautiful features.

"Hi, Franny. Did I catch you at an inconvenient time?" I hope I've missed the morning rush.

"No, come in."

"Can I get you anything? Those bar cookies are cool enough to eat." She angles her head toward the racks by a long marble counter in the center of the room. There's a citrusy lemon scent in the warm air from the ovens.

I hesitate for a second but shake my head. I ate too much at the picnic the other day and I'm still trying to make up for it. Once I had gotten over my anger with Ian, I'd actually had a good time meeting his family. Surprisingly, he hadn't taken the opportunity to ask me out again when he brought Drew and me home that night.

I wasn't disappointed in the least.

"The reason I dropped by was because I feel like you were hurt when you found out about Drew."

She frowns and runs her fingers over the counter. "I admit I was a little. I mean, you're one of my bridesmaids, and I didn't even know you had a brother, let alone one who lives with you. Maybe that's on me. Maybe I'm such an awful friend I never asked enough questions about your personal life because I've been caught up in my own. If that's the case, I'm sorry."

"Please don't apologize. I came here to apologize to you. You're one of the least self-centered people I know."

"Then why?"

Blowing out a breath, I fold my arms in front of me and lean against the counter. "It's hard to explain, but I've been thinking about it a lot lately. I think a lot of it is habit. I tend to deflect and change the subject when conversations get personal. Part of it is to avoid explanations. A major part has always been to protect Drew. And if I'm being honest, it's part of my armor too."

She nibbles on her lip and nods. "I can understand that."

"Please know it is in no way a reflection on you or our friendship."

"Okay. Friendships have never been easy for me. I've always been the shy, awkward girl who avoided people. I'm sure you're aware of some of that. Joining book club with you and the girls and then the small business meetings you convinced me to attend were major milestones for me. I was an anxious mess over them in the beginning, but now they're so important to me. You're important to me. I want to be as good a friend to you as you've been to me this past year."

"Well, shit, Franny." Tears fill my eyes, and I clear my throat. "You have been a good friend. I was thrilled when you asked me to be your bridesmaid."

Franny steps forward and gives me a hug. I give her a quick squeeze and pull back to wipe my eyes. Great, now I'll look like a drunk raccoon and have to fix my makeup before I open my shop this morning.

"My parents died in a helicopter crash while on vacation when I was twenty-two. It was a bit of a late honeymoon for them since they had never had one. They got pregnant with me really young. Drew was another surprise baby—thirteen years after I came along."

She rubs my shoulder. "I'm so sorry."

"You probably noticed Drew has some developmental delays."

"I noticed he's really sweet and his maturity level is a little lower than other teenage boys."

I smile. "He is really sweet most of the time. He's on the autism spectrum and he has various learning disabilities. One of those was selective mutism when he was younger. He would shut down or get agitated when people were around. That, coupled with losing our parents, made it easier to isolate ourselves."

"He seemed pretty comfortable with us the other day. Did he grow out of it?"

"Mostly, yes. He genuinely enjoys meeting people now. Certain situations trigger his anxiety, but like I said, it's become a habit to keep private."

She lays her hand on my arm. "I understand. I'm really glad you told me. I hated feeling like I hadn't been a good friend to you. That you hadn't felt comfortable sharing such an important part of your life. I was trying to come up with a way to talk to you about it. As you may have noticed, I like to plan things out. I'm not impulsive."

"Impulsivity is highly overrated. I've gotten into trouble the few times I've given in to the urge. I'm a planner. It's important for Drew to have routines."

She purses her lips. "Does one of those impulsive times involve Ian? You've never told me what happened between you two."

I squeeze my eyes shut and grimace. "You know that one-night stand I mentioned at a book club a while back?"

Franny eyes get wide, and she bites her lip. "I was wondering if that was Ian, but I was afraid to ask. It didn't go well? I mean, obviously it did for him because he flirts with you a lot."

I roll my eyes. "He's just a born flirt."

"Uh-huh. Ian is charming, but he's different with you. Lots of sparks flying between you two."

I cover my eyes with my hand and peek at her through my open fingers. "It happened in Boston before I moved here. I had signed the papers on the building and was heading back to New York, but since I had finished a day early and Drew was at my cousin's house, I decided to stay over in Boston and celebrate. I met Ian at the bar in the hotel, and, well…let's just say I'd had a long dry spell and decided what could one little night of sex with a hot stranger hurt. Little did I know when I moved here a few months later I would run into that one-night stand living here in his hometown."

"What are the odds of that happening?"

I drop my hand and give her a dry look. "Tell me about it. I nearly had a stroke when I walked into my first small business group meeting and there he was."

"What was his reaction?"

"He gave me a long stare and then the corner of his mouth lifted in that annoying smirk of his. He's been punishing me ever since."

"Punishing you for what?"

"It may have something to do with me sneaking out of his hotel room in the middle of the night while he was in the bathroom. He started asking me personal questions like my last name and where I was from and suggested spending the day together. I panicked and ran."

Her mouth opens and closes, then her eyebrows scrunch together. "I can't believe I'm asking this, but was he that bad in bed?"

My skin flushes and I clamp my hands under my arms so I won't fan my cheeks and draw attention to them.

A little smirk flits across her lips. "Or was he so good and that's why you panicked and ran?"

I tilt my head back and stare at the ceiling. Yes, he was damn good. Mind-blowingly good. He knows just how to touch a woman in all the right places in all the right ways.

Franny clears her throat and fans her face dramatically. "I feel like we should drink glasses of wine or brandy or cognac while having this conversation."

"You don't even drink."

"I know, but this moment seems to call for it. I don't smoke either, but it feels appropriate to be puffing on a cigarette or a cigar too. Like in an old black-and-white film where you don't actually see anything happening but their body language tells you something really passionate occurred."

A chuckle turns into a snort as I imagine us drinking wine and blowing smoke rings in the air. Franny giggles and then hiccups as we fall against each other laughing with tears in our eyes.

"Um, should I come back later?"

I glance over my shoulder at Olivia standing in the archway between the kitchen and the front of the store with a curious smile on her face. I wave her over.

"Franny has decided to take up drinking and smoking."

Olivia stops in front of us and grins. "If I didn't know any better, I'd say both of you have been imbibing this morning."

"I think I might need to take an early lunch and go visit my fiancé. Olivia, you can hold down the bakery for an hour or two or three, can't you?"

Olivia folds her arms over her waist. "Now I really want to know what you two were talking about. Or maybe not, because we both can't take a long early lunch to visit our fiancés."

I give them the evil-eye glare. "I hate you both right now."

Franny plants a hand on her hip and raises her eyebrows. "I happen to know someone who would be more than happy to scratch that itch for you."

"Bitch." I stick my tongue out at her, and she laughs.

"Stop torturing me. Who and what are we talking about? On second thought, I'm pretty sure I can guess the what but do I know the who?"

Franny glances at me, and I roll my eyes and sigh. "She's referring to Ian Flannigan and the one-night stand I had with him in Boston before I moved here."

"Oh, my. He is a handsome one, isn't he? So, are you thinking of picking up where you left off?"

"No, I don't do relationships. That's why I thought a stranger in a strange city was safe."

"Why don't you do relationships?" Olivia tilts her head, and her face scrunches in concern.

She's happily in love just like Franny. They probably can't imagine someone not wanting the relationship bliss they're in. But my experience with relationships is far from blissful.

"My plate is full. I don't have the time or energy to devote to another individual right now."

"Love happens when and where you least expect it."

"Not if you take the proper precautions. Like not date at all."

They both gape at me like I'm crazy to avoid the chance of love. They're both in the newly-in-love, everything-is-perfect phase. They've forgotten there's another side effect of relationships—a painful one.

Loving hurts.

CHAPTER 10

on't do it. Walk away and go home. Take a nice long bubbly bath and have a large glass of wine.

A couple skirts around me and enters Flannigan's Pub while I pretend to stare at the menu behind the glass case outside the double wooden doors. It's a Saturday night and the place is busy. Music and conversation drift out of the three-story building. People sit at the tables in front of the large bay windows flanking the doors. They're probably wondering what can be so interesting about the menu that has kept me staring at it for the past five minutes. Either that, or they assume I'm an exceedingly slow reader. Or the truth, that I can't decide whether to go in or do the sensible thing and go home.

I have to work in the morning.

Not until eleven though.

Most importantly, Drew is at my cousin Jane's for the weekend. Franny's bridal shower was this evening, so I had to make arrangements. My cousin picked him up this morning. I met her halfway in Massachusetts so she only had to drive an hour and a half each way and not make the six-hour round trip between upstate New York and New Hampshire. It happens once or twice a year and feels like my

NO CHOICE AT ALL

birthday and Christmas at the same time, even though I'm a Scorpio and my birthday is in November.

This is my one opportunity to do something just for me—possibly for an entire year.

I grab the brass bar on the door and swing it open. Just because I go inside doesn't mean I have to make my decision yet. Ian might not even be here tonight.

He might have lost interest.

I haven't seen him since the party. He may have finally given up. Wouldn't that be a kick in the pants? Or dress. I glance down at the fire engine red dress I poured myself into. The three-inch red heels bring my height to six feet, and I look up and scan the room, able to see over most of the people milling around the polished wooden bar spanning almost the entire left side of the building. There are two bartenders behind the bar—neither of them Ian.

A waitress in black jeans and a royal blue polo with Flannigan's Pub scrawled across her chest calls out to me from a nearby table, "There's room at the bar. If you're waiting for a table, it'll be a few minutes."

I nod absently.

A cacophony of sound from the flat screen televisions hanging on the walls, the rumble of conversations, and clinking of glasses and dishes surrounds me. The heavy scent of fried food from the booth by the door wrinkles my nose, and my mouth waters for the taste of a good old-fashioned basket of french fries. I glance at the table. No basket, but there is a heap of golden fries on a plate next to a burger bigger than my hand. Good, they're not the seasoned kind. I hate those. I should bring Drew some time for dinner—or get takeout. It might be too noisy in here for him.

A quick search of the booths lining the perimeter and the few tables in the center doesn't produce Ian either. Just my luck, he's not here. Maybe fate is telling me something.

Sighing, I turn to leave and catch sight of a familiar dark head in the corner of the bar where it wraps around. I step closer and angle my head for a better view. He's got one hand on the bar and the other on the back of a bar stool as he leans over a pair of very long bare tan legs crossed at the knee.

I grit my teeth and walk closer.

His profile comes into view. The straight nose, tanned skin, and grin are all the same. It's Ian. Long blonde hair flips over a shoulder, and the woman wraps her arms around his neck and pulls him in for a kiss.

The breath freezes in my lungs as my gaze locks on the pair entangled in a scorching embrace bordering on public indecency.

I spin away and stride to the door. Fate is a nasty bitch.

My shoes thump as I stomp down the sidewalk. My feet will pay the price later.

I knew he was a player. I knew I was simply one of the masses.

Stomp. Stomp. Stomp.

What the hell was I thinking coming here tonight? Shadows play across the sidewalk from the streetlights and headlights passing by.

The back of my shoe grates against my heel. I'll have a monster-sized blister by the time I reach my apartment.

Good. It's what I deserve for being so stupid.

"Glad it's not me you're ready to murder this time. Who or what has pissed you off this time, killer?"

I snap my head up. Ian is walking toward me down the sidewalk. I stop.

I glance behind me to Flannigan's Pub almost two blocks back. How did he get from the pub to down the street and walking in the opposite direction?

He stops in front of me with his hands stuffed in the pockets of his trousers. He's not breathing heavily. He couldn't have run down the back of the buildings along the parking lot next to the docks to intercept me. Besides, why would he bother?

"Cat got your tongue?"

"How did you get from your pub to here so fast?"

Ian glances over my shoulder toward his pub. A smile quirks up the corner of his mouth. "You were in my pub?" His smile turns into a grin. "I'm wearing you down, aren't I?"

I raise my chin and plant a hand on my hip. "Don't flatter yourself. I simply went in for a drink and saw you performing exploratory dental surgery with your tongue on a blonde."

His grin widens. "Jealous, Rebecca?"

I narrow my eyes and open my mouth to blast him. He holds up a hand and chuckles.

"Hold it. Before you slice into me with that razor sharp tongue of yours—you must have seen my brother Ryan. My twin brother. He's in town visiting. Since he missed the anniversary party because of work conflicts, he flew in a couple of days ago."

I'd met two of his brothers, Mike and Conner, at the party. No one had mentioned the missing brother was Ian's twin.

His shirt is green. The shirt on the man in the bar had been black.

My anger deflates like a ruptured balloon.

He's right. I acted like I was jealous of seeing him with another woman. Heat blazes over my skin, and I step away from the overhead streetlight and into the shadow of the closest building to hide the evidence of my blush. I fold my arms in front of me and look up and down the street, waiting for the cool night air to cool my overheated skin and for a plausible excuse to jump into my brain.

I wasn't jealous. I was simply disappointed my plans to have a second one-night stand were ruined.

Ian props a hand on the building over my head and leans in so close a hint of aftershave or cologne coming off his skin fills my nose. Or maybe the scent is just him.

"Why were you in my bar, Rebecca?"

I glare at the gap of tanned skin revealed at his throat by the top button of his shirt being undone. "I told you I wanted a drink."

"You came into my bar for a drink dressed like that?"

I peer up and meet his gaze. A completely different heat pools in my core as his blue gaze travels over my body and rests on my lips.

"What's wrong with the way I'm dressed?"

"Not a single thing. You're sexy as fuck."

"Crass." I lift my chin, look away, and pretend the tiny zip of lightning speeding along my nerves has nothing to do with pleasure.

"Your brother is better-looking than you. If he's not serious about that blonde at the bar, have him call me." I step around him and take two steps down the sidewalk before he grabs my hand, bringing me to a halt.

"Over my dead body."

He grips my hand tightly, but not so tight I can't pull away. His lowered brow and narrowed gaze make me smirk.

"Jealous, Ian?"

"Damn straight. I've made no secret of my interest in you. I'll be damned if I'll sit back and let you go out with my brother."

Why the hell does that send a thrill coursing through me?

The smirk dies instantly, and I frown.

My plan to scratch an itch and end his chase suddenly seems like a terrible idea.

"What's going through that beautiful head of yours?" He tugs on my hand.

I step closer and lay my free hand flat on his chest. The warmth of his skin radiates through the thin cotton of his shirt to my palm.

"What if I proposed a second no-strings-attached night together?"

He skims his hand along my waist to my back and pulls me flush against his body.

"I'd say I'm ready whenever and wherever you are."

The erection thickening and lengthening against my abdomen makes it very clear he's ready now. I swallow and flex my fingers against his chest.

He places my hand on his shoulder and wraps a second arm around my back, arching me even closer to his aroused body.

His lips brush my forehead and temple. Then whisper across my cheek and behind my ear.

A shiver of pleasure tingles down my spine, and I close my eyes.

He shifts and backs me into the alcove of the shop next to us while his lips continue down my neck and back up.

I turn my head slightly toward his lips grazing over my cheek, and he kisses me.

66

I clutch his shoulder and sigh into his mouth as his tongue parts my lips.

It's been so long since I've been kissed. Almost two years. Since that one night with Ian.

His tongue duels with mine. His lips caress and capture mine as his hands roam over my back and hips.

The cold brick of the building chills my shoulders as I gasp and lean back.

Ian's lips and tongue work their way down my neck to the dip of my shoulder. Cool air follows the warmth of his mouth, touching every place on my skin that he's touched.

"Your place or mine, sweetheart?"

Hmm? Oh, I hadn't thought this far ahead. Mine's probably closer. Unless Ian lives over his pub. In that case, they're probably equal distance.

Wait. Does he live over his pub?

I pull my head away from his mouth so I can think properly.

"Where do you live? Over your pub?"

I don't really want him in my bed because then every time I climb into bed, I'll have his image there. Distance is better. Then I can leave and forget all about it.

He shakes his head and kisses me again.

"Five minutes away."

Our tongues dance together as his hand slides up and cups my breast. I melt into his hand.

"Ten minutes tops."

Too far.

"My place," I whisper as I push him back a step.

If his presence lingers past the night, I can always dispose of all my bedding and buy new. I'll make room in the budget. I have emergency savings. This qualifies as an emergency, doesn't it?

Sirens wail in the distance. We both turn our heads toward the sound just as Ian's phone rings. He frowns and pulls it from his pocket.

"It's the pub. This should only take a second."

He keeps a hand on my waist as he answers the phone. The sirens grow louder. They're coming this way.

Ian lowers the phone with a grimace. "There's a fire in the pub's kitchen. I have to go."

"Of course, go."

Lights flash over the hill into the village.

He cups my face in his palms and kisses me. "This isn't over." He looks over his shoulder toward my building. "I don't like leaving you on the street."

"Go, Ian. I'll be fine."

He sprints down the sidewalk to Flannigan's. There's a crowd of people gathered outside the pub—the patrons and probably a few curious onlookers.

The siren at the firehouse on top of the hill blares, and the garage doors rise.

Ian disappears down the road next to his building. He's probably going directly to the kitchen. I take a step toward the pub. What if he needs help?

I stop and shake my head. What help could I provide? I turn and walk away with my arms around my waist. The chill of the night seeps into my skin as a police vehicle and a firetruck pull up in front.

I was right. Fate really is a nasty bitch.

CHAPTER 11

I sip at my third—maybe fourth—cup of coffee as I drum my fingers on the counter. I haven't been able to sum up the energy to do much more than wait on the customers that trickled in today. I stared out my window until the flashing lights had disappeared last night, then I tossed and turned for hours. Some special night it had turned out to be—not.

From the bits and pieces of gossip local customers shared, I pieced together it had been a grease fire that had quickly been snuffed out with no one hurt. Lucky, but I imagine Ian still had his hands full dealing with the emergency and the cleanup.

Speak of the devil, and he appears.

Ian walks into my shop with a cup of coffee in each hand. I take a second to marvel he opened the door without dropping a cup or spilling any of their contents. His hair is damp and curls against his neck. Straight from the shower?

"Morning." His blue eyes gaze around the shop and then land back on me. "Brought you a coffee. Franny told me it was your favorite." He glances at the mug clutched in my hands. "I guess you don't need it."

"On the contrary. Gimme." I plop my mediocre coffee on the counter and reach with both hands for the cup in his hand.

He chuckles, holds the cup out to the side, and leans forward over the counter. "Pay the toll first, beautiful."

I stare at his waiting lips and then the coffee. While I tossed and turned last night, I concluded the fire had saved me from another poor impulsive decision. I need to go back to putting distance between Ian and me.

But I really want that coffee.

"Franny said it was my favorite? Caramel macchiato?"

"Damn, you're hell on a guy's ego, killer. You're leaving me hanging with my lips puckered to grill me on the coffee? Yeah, it's whatever you just said."

I frown, buss him absently on the lips, and grab the coffee out of his hand.

He shakes his head and sips at his own while I clutch the cup in both hands and hold it to my lips, closing my eyes and inhaling the scent before slowly taking a sip against the tip of my tongue to make sure it's not too hot.

Ian groans, and I pop my eyes open.

"Never thought I'd be jealous of coffee before."

"It's amazing coffee." I take a full sip, and my lips lower in bliss as it slides over my tongue and down my throat. Creamy dark deliciousness with just the right kick of caffeine.

He's watching my face intently. I clear my throat. "The gossip mill says it was a grease fire?"

"Yeah. Joe, a new employee, was handling the fryolator last night, and he didn't pay attention. Ron, my chef, got it put out before it did any damage beyond a lot of smoke and panic."

"Then you're all clear to open?"

"The smoke was gone by the time I left this morning. There was still the smell, but I think that was just me. I went home and showered, caught a couple hours of sleep, then showered again when I thought I caught the smell of smoke again. Might've just been my imagination though." He leans closer. "What do you think?"

I start to lean forward then rear back. "I'm not sniffing you."

"Come on, help a guy out. I don't want to go around reeking of smoke."

I inhale slightly without leaning forward. There's no trace of smoke I can detect—a fresh scent like after a heavy rain mixed with a hint of beach and the sea. I inch closer and inhale deeper before I catch myself and step back from the counter and drink my coffee.

"You're fine. No smoke."

He folds his arms on top of the counter. "How does tonight work for a makeup for last night?"

"It doesn't."

"You're not backing out on me, are you, beautiful?"

"It was a onetime offer."

Ian hangs his head and sighs. "I'm firing that kid."

"What kid?"

"Joe, the one that started the damn fire."

"Well, he did start a fire, but don't fire him because of me."

"I had decided to give him another shot, but my mood has suddenly soured."

"Look, it was an impulsive decision last night. Luckily, circumstances intervened and prevented us from making a mistake."

"Why would it be a mistake?"

"Because we live in the same town and cross paths on numerous occasions. One-night stands are for strangers who will never see each other again."

"Says who?"

"Me."

"How did that work out for you the first time?"

"Badly, which is exactly why it's not a good idea."

"And who says circumstances didn't intervene that time and make sure we ended up living in the same town so we could do it again?"

I narrow my eyes. I hate when my words are used against me.

"Come on, killer. Let me have another chance at our second night." He winks. "I guarantee to remove all possibility of any interruptions."

I sigh and shake my head. "First, I think that's probably impossible.

Second, last night was my one free night for the foreseeable future. Drew is at my cousin's house in New York. I have to go pick him up after work. It probably won't happen again for months if not until next year."

He frowns and straightens. "There's no one else to watch him?"

"No."

"And if I come up with a viable solution?"

"What does that mean?" I wave my hand. "Never mind. No."

"If I can find a suitable sitter for the night or any time of day that works for you?"

I shake my head. "No, I'm not leaving Drew with a stranger. Like I said, last night was a onetime offer which has expired. It's for the best." Jane is the only one who's ever watched him over night. I'm not arranging another sleepover which involves several hours of driving for a booty call.

"I vehemently disagree."

"Too bad. Besides, the urge has passed."

"Let's see about that." He waltzes around the counter.

I throw up my hand. "Stop right there."

"Why? If the urge has truly passed, then what are you afraid of?" He stops in front of me and raises his hand to cup my cheek.

"This is my place of business," I hiss at him. "Anyone could walk in."

"So?"

"So, I wish to portray more professionalism than you obviously do, and I'm not interested in becoming a topic of gossip."

He sighs heavily and drops his forehead against mine.

I glance toward the door and step back. His hand falls away.

"Okay, how about dinner? Can you get a sitter for a few hours instead of all night?"

"I don't see the point."

"We can discuss it at dinner."

A logical, candid discussion might be what's needed for both of us to move on and put this all behind us.

"Dinner where? I don't want to be seen in town. It will raise questions and gossip. You know how small towns are."

"We can go outside of town, or you can come to my place."

Nope, absolutely not. I'm not going to his house. We're meeting in a public place where there's no chance of anything happening beyond a conversation that brings closure to this non-relationship.

"Restaurant."

"When?"

I sip my coffee and run over my schedule in my head. "I'll have to see when Corinne is available."

"Okay, who's Corinne?"

"She's a special education teacher at a school in a neighboring town who was recommended to me as a sitter by the special needs parents' group in town. She watches him once or twice a month for a few hours so I can attend book club and small business group meetings." She's saved my sanity.

"Name the day and time and I'll make it work."

"You do realize this is just to meet and have a conversation about all the reasons this won't work between us, right?"

"I realize that's what you plan to talk about. I will, of course, be giving you all the reasons it can work perfectly."

This is probably another bad idea. I seem to have a lot of them lately.

Ian kisses me while I frown down at my coffee cup.

"Stop doing that!"

He smirks. "Why? I enjoy kissing you."

"Kissing is not part of the discussion. At least not kissing outside of the onetime event which might, or most likely not, take place. A no-strings one-night stand does not involve kissing hello and goodbye or any other time apart from the one event."

His eyebrows have climbed higher and higher up his forehead, and his smirk has grown more pronounced as he stares down at me.

"What is wrong with you? This should be a guy's wet dream—no-strings sex—no tangled relationship worries. Why are you making it complicated?"

He laughs. "Are you questioning my manhood?" He grasps my hips and yanks me against him. "I can prove to you quite thoroughly that

I'm a man." His breath whispers over my ear. "Shame on you for perpetuating gender stereotypes, killer."

I drop my head to his chest and groan. "You drive me crazy."

"The feeling is mutual, beautiful." He kisses the top of my head.

"What about Friday? Fridays usually work for Corinne."

"I'll make it work. Does this mean you'll finally give me your phone number?"

"I shouldn't," I mumble with my head still nestled against his chest.

"Show me how brave you are."

I sigh and rattle off my phone number.

He enters it into his phone and winks. "That wasn't so hard, was it?"

I step away from him and polish off my coffee. I've had so much caffeine today I'll probably start twitching.

My phone vibrates on the counter. I glance over. He's sent me his contact information with a smiley face.

I roll my eyes. "You better not start texting me with emojis. I hate emojis."

"What do you have against emojis? They save a lot of time, and they're cute."

"Cute?"

"You're not going to question my masculinity again, are you?" He steps close to me as I back into the counter.

"That depends on whether you're going to send me little hearts and smiley faces."

He grins and places a hand on either side of me on the counter, caging me in. "I think I can be a little more original than that. You're going to love receiving texts from me. It's going to be the highlight of your day."

I raise my chin and one eyebrow. "There goes that ego again."

His cheek skims mine as he lowers his head and whispers in my ear, "Shall we make a bet?"

The hair on my arms and nape lift. My fingers tremble, so I stuff them behind me between the counter and my back. "What are the terms?"

His lips brush against my ear. "For every smile I drag out of you with a text, you owe me a date."

A shiver of pleasure tingles down from my ear to my core. "And what do I get when your texts leave me...unimpressed and unsmiling?"

He lifts his head. "What do you want?" His gaze drops to my lips. "How about a kiss for every text that fails to make you smile?"

"Uh, no. If your text doesn't make me smile, then you can't text me or show up for an entire day."

"Aw, come on, killer. That's harsh."

"We could make it a week. After all, you're asking for a date for each twitch of my lips."

"Fine, but you'd miss me too much. Besides, you're going to be smiling a lot." He taps the end of my nose with his finger. "Can I trust you to be honest?"

"I'm a Scorpio. Honesty is in my DNA."

"Then it's a deal." His lips capture mine. Before I can protest, he turns and walks around the counter. "Talk soon, beautiful."

I lick my lips. He likes his coffee sweet.

Ian walks out the door and disappears down the sidewalk. I prop my hip against the counter and fold my arms in front of me. My phone buzzes behind me.

A unicorn with hearts for eyes, a kitten, a puppy, and a bunny appear on the screen.

I smile and shake my head.

There's a knock on the front window. Ian holds up his index finger and mouths, "That's one date."

Damn it! Who doesn't smile at bunnies and unicorns?

CHAPTER 12

"To be clear, this does not count as the date you owe me for from our bet. This was already arranged before the bet took place." Ian opens the door of his Jeep for me.

"Understood, counselor."

He chuckles behind me as I climb into the passenger seat and arrange the skirt of my navy blue suit over my legs. Maybe I should have changed out of my work outfit, but time was limited and I didn't want to look like I was putting too much effort into our dinner.

I already had to school my expression every time my phone went off so I wouldn't lose more during our bet. He had stayed away all week because he lost on the last two texts. Every time the phone beeped or buzzed with an incoming text, I thought of things that made me sad or angry before looking at my phone. Worked like a charm.

He pulls the seatbelt across me, brushing against my breasts and hip, before he snaps it into place.

"I'm perfectly capable of fastening my own seatbelt." I stare at the way his light blue dress shirt pulls tight over his biceps as he leans over me.

"I know." He leans forward and kisses me. "Hi, beautiful."

He hadn't kissed me hello when I answered the door. He'd given me a wink and a grin before Drew had monopolized his attention for the next ten minutes while I talked to Corinne and told her exactly where we would be.

There wasn't a shred of disappointment when he hadn't kissed me. Not even the slightest twinge.

Okay, maybe a twinge.

Besides, if he had, then I might have to explain to Drew about our relationship. I told Corinne it was a business dinner, and as soon as we discuss the summer business fair over dinner, it will be.

His lips linger on mine for another kiss and then another.

I'm going to push him away any minute now.

"Miss me?"

His blue eyes are inches from mine. It's like staring into tiny whirlpools of the Caribbean Sea. Hypnotizing.

I blink. "Nope."

Okay, that might be a tiny white lie.

He grins like he can read my mind and gives me another quick kiss before backing out of the Jeep and closing the door.

While he walks around the front of the vehicle, I take a deep breath. This dinner is not the beginning of anything–it's the end. We'll have an adult conversation about the merits of maintaining a friendship and a professional working relationship. Neither of which includes kissing.

My phone buzzes, and I pull it from my purse. Is it Corinne? Has something happened with Drew already? Is he upset I left?

A short video of kittens climbing all over a dog while he lies quietly in his bed plays on my screen. I smile.

He opens the driver side door. "That's two dates."

"Wait a minute. This is cheating! It's not emojis."

"Our bet was for texts. We didn't stipulate the texts had to be emojis."

I narrow my eyes at him as he grins. How am I not supposed to smile at kittens?

"Fine, but the bet is over."

"Don't tell me you're a sore loser?"

"I am not, but the bet can't go on indefinitely. It makes sense to set tonight as the end date. You've got two dates out of it. Be satisfied with that."

"I'll agree the bet will end tonight. But at the end of tonight."

If I block his number, will he consider it cheating? I can't turn off my phone in case Drew needs me. A date is only a few hours at most. He can't win too many more out of me in that time. "I can live with that."

He starts the vehicle and backs out of the parking space. "You know, I looked up Scorpios."

"Excuse me?"

"You said you were a Scorpio, so I looked it up."

"Okay..."

"Do you know Scorpios are highly compatible with those born under the Taurus sign?"

"Let me guess, you're a Taurus?"

"Sure am. According to the astrological experts, we're a highly passionate match with combustible sexual chemistry."

"You're making that up."

"Nope. Look it up yourself."

I pick up my phone and do a search. "It says we're polar opposites." Isn't that the truth?

"Keep reading."

Fascinated and frustrated by one another. Difficult to form a relationship, but once they do, it's long-lasting. I put down my phone. "You're into astrology?"

"I am now."

I sense his gaze on me as I look out the window at Granite Cove disappearing behind us in the side mirror.

"You're not going to keep reading? Interesting stuff in there."

"I'm sure there is. I get carsick if I read too much."

"Wouldn't want that. This place we're going to has the best seafood around."

"And what if I told you I'm allergic to seafood?"

"Then we'll go somewhere else. Tell me what you like."

"Seafood."

He chuckles. "Any actual allergies I should know about?"

"No, not a single one."

"Good to know. Me neither. Makes life a little easier."

"I guess."

"Why are you so quiet all of a sudden?"

I gaze at his profile.

He glances at me and then back to the road. "Talk to me, beautiful. You make me nervous when you get quiet."

"Why?"

"Because it usually means you're thinking too much and you're going to come up with reasons this is a bad idea."

"It is a bad idea."

"I don't believe in bad ideas. All ideas are good ones. It's the implementation where things can go awry."

"I don't date, Ian. I have a firm rule about it. Yet here I am on a date with you and I've agreed to two more because of that bet."

"Okay, why do you have that rule?"

"Because I'm not looking for a relationship. I don't have the time or the emotional resources to deal with one right now."

"We've had fun together so far, right?"

"That's not the point."

"It should be. I like being with you. I sure as hell like having sex with you and really want to again. I'm not asking you to marry me, Rebecca."

Am I overthinking this? I want to have sex with him again too. That's the problem, isn't it? I can't afford to get attached to Ian. Sex is one thing. Dates and sex are something else entirely.

"You offered no-strings-attached sex."

"I offered one time of no-strings-attached sex. You've turned it into three dates."

"I haven't added any strings to it. It's still no-strings-attached. You're not committed to anything. I'll let you choose the time and place of the dates. There's no time pressure. And the emotional part is entirely up to you. You put in as much or as little as you want. Deal?"

He's being accommodating. There's no reason to be wary. I am overthinking this. A casual no-strings affair is exactly what I can handle. No commitment. No obligations. And on my own schedule. What more could I ask for?

CHAPTER 13

*S*heets changed—check.

Legs and other body parts shaved—check.

Sexy black lingerie on under my easy-to-remove wrap dress —check.

The frittata is warming in the oven. Fresh juice and coffee are prepared. Drew is off to school. All that remains is Ian's arrival.

He'd given me a small smile that slowly stretched into a grin after our date on Friday when I'd invited him over for Monday breakfast. That grin had replayed in my head the entire weekend, prompting butterflies in my tummy and heat waves over my skin. Either that or I'm going through the change of life at thirty.

Mondays are the only day when both Blossoms is closed and Drew is at school. If I'm to fit in those four dates he won with our bet, I'll need to get creative. I still can't believe he won another one during our date. Damn laughing babies GIFs.

With this invite, I'll owe only three more dates, and if all goes well and we both get our itches scratched, maybe all this built-up sexual tension will go away. It's only because it's been so long since I've had sex. That one night with Ian couldn't possibly be as good as I remember. Having a second time will prove that and allow us both to move on. End of story.

The date had actually been enjoyable. He hadn't pressured me about setting up future dates, and he'd been charming and entertaining. The food had been fantastic. I didn't regret using one of my precious babysitting nights for it.

The outside stairs creak, and my heart picks up speed. There's no reason to be nervous. Sex has never made me nervous. It's a natural body function.

There's a hard rap against the apartment door. I jump.

I wrap my fingers over the back of the stool, hang my head, and take a breath.

I am a smart, powerful woman. I decide. This is my choice. I can change my mind at any time.

I stride to the door and swing it open. Ian's gaze rolls over me and he whistles. I do the same to him minus the whistle, taking in his black pants and turquoise polo.

"Morning, beautiful." He leans down and hesitates. "Okay if I kiss you?"

I snatch the front of his shirt and pull his lips to mine.

His chuckle ends as soon as our lips meet. He swings the door shut behind him and cups my face in his hands, exploring my mouth with his tongue.

I wrap my arms around his neck and delve my fingers into his thick hair. I nip his bottom lip.

Ian groans and backs me up against the hallway wall. His hands slide down my sides and grip my waist.

I suck his tongue into my mouth and wrap my leg over his hip. His hands clench my waist then slip over my ass and press me against him. I gasp and push back with my hips.

We begin a slow dance of friction as our mouths devour one another.

His chest heaves as I press my hands over his pecs, down his abdomen, and around his sides to his back.

He grips my thigh and raises my leg higher, angling our bodies for a tighter fit. My breath stutters. Heat and pleasure race over my skin and pool low in my core.

I might orgasm from only this.

His hand slides up under my dress and over my hip. I drop my head to his shoulder and pant. His mouth trails down my neck, licking and nipping my skin.

He lifts me, and I wrap both legs around his waist.

"Where's the bedroom, baby? We need a bed for what I want to do to you."

He kisses along my jaw as I point to my room down the hall. He turns and strides toward it with me in his arms. I clutch his shoulders and moan. Every step he takes rubs our bodies together, sensitizing every inch of my skin.

Ian lays me on my bed, and I scramble to untie my dress. My hands shake. The laces tighten instead of loosening beneath my fumbling fingers. I get myself under control and untie the laces.

The dress falls open. I look up. Ian has removed his shirt, but his hands are frozen on the button of his pants. His gaze rakes over me.

"You are so damn beautiful."

I keep my gaze locked on his as I sit up and knock his hands out of the way to unfasten his pants. He tucks my hair behind my ear and runs his fingers along the edge of my jaw. His thumb presses against my lower lip and I kiss the tip.

"Lie down, sweetheart." His voice is guttural and full of arousal.

I slip my arms out of my dress and follow his direction, lying back as he strips off the rest of his clothes and climbs up the bed over me.

He kisses me as his hands survey my body. The weight and heat of him is like a luxurious aphrodisiac.

He unhooks my bra and grins down at my breasts. "It's better than opening presents on Christmas morning."

I laugh as his head lowers to my chest. The laughter stops abruptly when his mouth closes over my nipple.

His hands leave no patch of skin untouched as he brushes them across my abdomen and down my legs, removing my panties.

My hands clench and unclench on his shoulders. His fingers trail up my thigh and concentrate where I need him the most. My thoughts scatter, and I clasp his head to my breast.

The orgasm builds in my core, then explodes and radiates across my nerve endings as I cry out. My toes curl and my belly quivers.

Ian's hands and mouth soothe me while I sink into the bed.

There's a rustle of plastic next to me and his weight shifts off me for a moment. My eyelids are too heavy to open.

His warmth and weight return, and I pry open my lids as I run my hands over his arms and shoulders. His tongue licks at my lips, seeking entrance that I eagerly grant.

As he fills me, he issues a harsh groan. I wrap my arms and legs around him.

I gasp for breath as the pleasure soars again.

He buries his head against my throat and clutches me against him as he surges inside me.

It's as if my body is hurtling toward the stars and detonating into space.

We remain wrapped in each other's arms as we come back to earth. He peppers my neck and shoulder with soft kisses.

"Do I still get breakfast? I'm starving."

I smack him on the shoulder. "Yes. The frittata is in the oven."

He chuckles and raises his head. "Food and sex. This may be the most perfect morning ever."

"That simple, are you?"

"Yup. Guys are pretty basic. We think about food or sex. When one is satisfied, our brains focus on the other until that one is satisfied. Then it starts all over again. Having both satisfied is nirvana."

"Women are more complicated."

He sighs. "Don't I know it." He rolls off the bed and saunters across the hall into the bathroom.

CHAPTER 14

"*A*ny chance you're free for lunch?"

Kelly fidgets in front of the counter. I glance around the shop.

"Now?"

She winces and shifts from side to side. "I know it's last minute. If you're too busy, I understand."

Cat is dusting the display shelves. I don't have any orders waiting. It's a Wednesday and not typically the busiest time of the week. Kelly brushes her bangs off her forehead and taps her fingers against her elbow. We're friendly. We chat at the business meetings and whenever we run into one another, but we've never gone to lunch. She seems upset.

"Let me talk to Cat really quick and then we can go, okay?"

Her shoulders drop. "Thanks."

I tell Cat I'm going out for lunch. She gives me an exaggerated surprised look only a teenager or a twenty-year-old can manage and then nods comically, glancing between Kelly and me. "Everything okay?"

"Yes. Just handle any customers. If you get busy, call me."

It's not like I've never left her in the shop alone before, but it wasn't to go to lunch. The few times I have it's been for Drew.

I grab my purse from underneath the counter and a cardigan in case it's too chilly. Kelly follows me out the front.

"Is it okay if we stay close? Cat is fine on her own, but I'd feel better if we didn't go far."

"Oh, no, that's perfect for me. I rarely leave my assistant alone, too, but it was either that or start screaming." She glances up and down the sidewalk.

"That might scare your customers away."

"It's the only reason I didn't."

"You want to tell me about it?" I look up the street. The streets are busy for the first week in May. "How about the Cove Café?"

She nods, and we walk up the sidewalk. The café is relatively small and serves only sandwiches and salads, but it's tasty and only two blocks away.

I glance at her walking next to me. The ends of her straight brown hair flap against her shoulders. Her purse hangs from her forearm extended by her side. Her posture is perfection.

"Were you a model?"

"What?"

I point up and down her body. "You walk like you're on a runway or something. I have to constantly remind myself to keep my shoulders back and head up."

"Oh, that's Mother's and Grandmother's training of me from birth. I was never a model, but thanks for the ego boost."

I chuckle. "So what has you ready to scream?"

She holds the door open for me as we reach the café. I step in and blink so my eyes adjust. There's a row of small metal tables against either wall. The space is narrow, but the cream-colored walls and big picture windows on either side of the door make it appear airy.

We walk to the back, where a young woman stands behind a wooden counter. The menu is on the wall behind her on a giant blackboard. She greets us with a smile. "What can I get for you today?"

After Kelly orders a cranberry and almond salad and I order a turkey and mango chutney sandwich, she insists on paying.

The woman gives us a little white triangle metal sign with a number on it. "Put this on your table and we'll bring your food over."

We pick an open table by one of the front windows. Kelly unfolds a napkin and smooths it over her lap. Her beige dress is form fitting. An intricate design is stitched along the collar and the ends of the sleeves.

"Did you make that dress?"

She glances down and then nods.

"It's beautiful."

"Thank you."

"I'm thirty-two years old and my parents still drive me crazy. Is that normal? Do your parents call you up daily and question every aspect of your life and every decision you make?"

I drop my gaze to the table. An ache builds in the center of my chest. "No, they don't. My parents passed away eight years ago."

Her mouth drops open and then she lowers her face into her hands. "I'm a thoughtless idiot. I'm so sorry."

"No, you're not. You didn't know, and besides, just because I no longer have my parents doesn't mean you don't get to complain about yours."

"Yes, it does." She drops her hands into her lap.

"Why?"

"Because it makes me realize the situation could be much worse and I should be thankful they're still around to drive me crazy."

"Well, there is that. Doesn't mean you can't vent though."

The server brings our drinks and tells us our order will be right out. I unfold my napkin and put it in my lap.

"Do they live here in town?"

"No, Chicago."

"Is that where you grew up?"

She nods and unscrews the cap from her water and takes a sip.

"How did you end up in Granite Cove?"

She snorts. "Closed my eyes and pointed on my map."

"You're joking!"

"No, I really did. I quit my job in New York and moved back home to Chicago. That lasted for a month before I knew I had to get out of there. I grabbed an old atlas off my parents' bookshelf and opened it randomly. I closed my eyes and pointed and here I am."

"Wow! I'm not an impulsive person. I can't imagine doing that." I did tons of research and reconnaissance before choosing Granite Cove. And lists—lots of lists.

Kelly shrugs. "I looked online and found a store for rent. My apartment was the only one I could afford that would also allow Waldo, my dog. It's worked out for the most part."

"Do your parents want you to move back to Chicago?"

"Among many other things, like settle down and pop out some grandchildren."

"Oh."

The food arrives, and I take a bite of my sandwich while Kelly pushes her salad around the plate with her fork. The sweet and tangy chutney complements the turkey and rye bread nicely.

"I feel like a failure when I get off the phone with them. I know that's not what they intend. They're really great parents." She closes her eyes.

"They don't understand the path you chose?"

"Definitely not. When I studied fashion in college, they wrung their hands and lectured me on backup plans. My father threw statistics at me. Lovingly, of course."

"I think my parents were too caught up with my brother to lecture me on what I studied." I shrug "Or maybe they trusted me to make the right decisions for myself. I thought I was going to be a CEO of a Fortune 500 company. Life has a way of changing when you least expect it."

"My siblings are all older, successful, and producing the required grandchildren. How old is your brother?"

"Drew is seventeen. I'm his guardian."

Kelly places her hand over her chest. Her mouth opens and closes.

"Oh, wow. I'm really stepping in it all over the place, aren't I? You must think I'm so shallow and selfish."

I shake my head. "Not in the least. Believe me, there are many times I want to scream. In hindsight, the cause ends up being rather trivial…or at least not as important as I felt at the time."

She tilts her head and wrinkles her brow. "I had no idea you had a brother living with you."

I smooth the napkin over my lap and sigh. "That's because I rarely share that information. Too private, I guess." Something I need to work on for Drew's sake and my own. What kind of message am I sending him by keeping us isolated?

"Thank you for sharing it with me and agreeing to lunch."

"It's not really lunch if you don't at least take a bite of that salad. I've already eaten half my sandwich."

Kelly laughs. "I'd rather have your sandwich. I don't know why I ordered the salad." She shakes her head. "Actually, I do. Because my grandmother got on the phone while I was talking to my parents and started telling me I should take up ballet to thin out my thighs."

I slide my plate over to her. "Be my guest."

"No, I couldn't. I'll order my own." She pushes the salad to the end of the table.

"Don't be silly. You'd be doing me a favor. If it sits in front of me, I will eat it even though I'm full. The size of this sandwich is more than enough for two people."

"Are you sure?"

"I wouldn't have offered if I wasn't."

"Thanks." She takes a bite and closes her eyes.

"You bought it anyway."

"This is superb."

I laugh and take a sip of my water. "I still need to fit in the bridesmaid dress, remember?"

She waves a hand over the plate. "It'll be perfect. You have nothing to worry about. Franny came in for her final fitting. She looks so beautiful."

"I can't believe the wedding is only a couple of weeks away."

"I know. I'm looking forward to it. I love weddings."

"I suppose that makes sense since you sell wedding gowns and attendant dresses."

"I hadn't planned to when I opened, but I had so many people come in and ask if I did, I checked into it. I ended up agreeing to do one wedding party, and it snowballed from there. Now it's half my business."

"It doesn't drive you crazy, dealing with all the emotional brides?"

"For the most part they're typical. Every once in a while I get a demanding customer, but I don't think it's confined to weddings. You should know. You design the flower arrangements."

"You're right. Personalities can be strong whether it's for a wedding or not."

"Speaking of forceful personalities..." Kelly gestures out the window with her water bottle.

Vanessa Michaels stalks down the sidewalk. Dark sunglasses hide her eyes, but her lips are compressed in a tight red line. Someone is going to be the target of her displeasure.

"She brought in a few outfits for me to tailor and accused me of ruining one of the dresses. There was a stain on the hem. I had never even touched the dress except to hang it in back."

"Please tell me you didn't give in to her."

"I did to keep the peace. She's the type of person who would have bad-mouthed me and my business to everyone. Now I make sure I check any garment thoroughly before I accept them from customers."

"She tried something similar with me when I first opened. She bought some flowers and came back the next week complaining they had died and accused me of using subpar suppliers."

"What did you do?"

"I informed her flowers die and if she wants them to last forever, she should invest in some quality silk flowers. I handed her a brochure on them I have at the shop."

Kelly throws her head back and laughs. "I wish I had the gumption to do something like that."

"Vanessa is the type of person who will walk all over you if you let her."

She tilts her head to the side and frowns. "She must be a very unhappy woman to derive so much pleasure from making others so miserable, don't you think?"

I snort. "I think you're kinder than I am. I just think she's an evil bitch."

Kelly points her finger at me. "That's possible too."

We both grin.

CHAPTER 15

I push the armchair into the corner and plop down with my legs hanging over one side and my torso resting against the opposite side. At this angle, I can watch the front of Flannigan's Pub. I haven't seen Ian since that Monday. He's keeping his word and letting me set the schedule.

Unfortunately, my plan to scratch an itch and be done didn't work. His face pops into my mind at the most inopportune times. Like when I was waiting on a customer who was telling me every single detail of her trip to Holland, including seeing the fields of tulips. Normally, I would find this interesting and I did, but then someone walked by the front of the store wearing a jacket almost the same color as his eyes, and my mind wandered. She asked me if I was listening three times.

Not one of my best moments.

I rest my head against the cool windowpane. It's not like I expect to see him walking in or out of his pub. He probably uses a back entrance like I do. So why am I sitting here staring at it instead of catching up on paperwork or getting a good night's sleep?

Something hits the window above my head with a thump. I lurch sideways and land on my ass on the floor.

Rubbing my posterior, I climb to my feet. Was it a bat? Birds don't fly at night, do they? Owls do—they're nocturnal.

I lean my forehead against the window, looking down at the sidewalk. *Please don't let there be a dead baby owl down there.*

Ian stands below my window with his hands in his pockets, grinning. I kneel on the chair, twist open the window, stick my head into the narrow opening, and hiss at him, "Are you crazy? What did you throw at my window—a rock?"

"It was a pebble, and why are you whispering?"

"Because Drew is asleep. What are you doing?"

"If you'd bother to answer your phone, I wouldn't have to resort to such methods. I saw you in the window."

My phone is in my bedroom, charging. Could he tell I was looking at his pub? That would be embarrassing, and he'd never let me live it down.

"I have a door, you know."

"Didn't think you'd let me in, but good to know." He walks toward the alleyway.

"Wait! Ian, get back here!"

He disappears around the corner of the building.

I scramble off the chair and dash to the door. His footsteps thump on the creaking stairs as I swing open the door.

His smile turns into a smirk as his gaze lingers on my yellow chick and white bunny pajamas. "Cute. Not what I pictured you sleeping in."

He rests a shoulder against the doorjamb. "Are you going to invite me in?"

"Just so we're clear, there's no hanky-panky going on. Drew is a light sleeper." I step back out of the opening.

"Hanky-panky? You're full of surprises tonight." He brushes by me and steals a kiss. "Hi, killer."

I sigh and close the door. Did I ask for this by daydreaming at the window, thinking of him? I snort. If it were that easy, I should've imagined a suitcase full of money.

Ian stands in the middle of my living room. He's wearing faded jeans torn at the knee and a white T-shirt that has seen better days.

He's sexy as hell when he's dressed in his standard pants and shirt, but dressed down like this? I want to drag him off to my bedroom.

"Penny for your thoughts?"

"My thoughts are worth a hell of a lot more than a penny."

He stalks closer, stopping inches from me. "Oh, yeah? Those must be interesting thoughts you're having, killer." His fingers trail up my bare arms. "Am I in them?"

I swat his hand away and walk over to the couch. "No touching." I crawl into the corner and grab a pillow, holding it in front of my chest.

He sits in the opposite corner. "What's the matter? Afraid you won't be able to control yourself?"

Yes. "Don't flatter yourself."

"I've missed you, beautiful. Did you miss me?"

"Did you go somewhere?"

He holds a hand over his heart. "You didn't even notice?" He stretches his arm across the back of the couch. "I was helping my brother move into his new place in Concord."

"Which brother?"

"Ryan."

"The more handsome twin?"

"You're a cruel woman, killer."

I place my hand on top of the couch, a few inches away from his. "I make no secret that I'm a bitch."

"You're not a bitch. You have thick armor and you use that wicked tongue of yours as a shield and weapon, but inside you're a marshmallow." The tips of his fingers touch mine.

I narrow my gaze. "I am not a marshmallow."

"A big, white, gooey center."

I whip the pillow at his head.

He ducks and bursts out laughing. The pillow bounces off him and onto the coffee table. I snatch it and wallop him with it.

"Shush! You'll wake up Drew." He grabs the pillow and tosses it away with one hand. With the other, he grabs my hand and pulls me into the crook of his arm.

I settle against him, and he wraps his arm over my shoulder and plays with the edge of my short-sleeved top.

He leans forward and plucks the remote off the table. "Will the TV wake him?"

"Not if we keep the volume below eighteen."

"That's pretty specific."

"I've tested it extensively."

He chuckles and turns on the TV. As he flips through the channels, I cross my legs and fold my arms in front of my waist. He stops on a crime drama and looks at me with one eyebrow raised. I shrug. He puts the remote down on the arm of the couch and grabs my hand, threading our fingers together, and rests them on his thigh.

I should scoot back over to my corner and put some distance between us. It's the wise thing to do.

Instead, I curl my legs up on the couch and snuggle into his shoulder.

I don't always want to be the wise one. The wise one doesn't get to have fun.

~

"WAKE UP, BABY."

I open my eyes. My head is on Ian's lap. His arm rests on top of mine. He brushes the hair off my cheek.

"It's late. As much as I would like to stay right here watching you sleep, I'm dozing myself. I figure you'd murder me if we both fell asleep and Drew found us in the morning."

Shit! I sit up and rub my hands over my cheeks.

"You thought right. What time is it?"

"After midnight."

He's leaning against the corner of the couch with his arm over the back, watching me.

"You snore."

"I do not!" Oh God, do I? It's been so many years since I slept with anyone, what if I do?

He smirks. "No, you don't."

He stands and holds out his hand. I take it, and he pulls me up into his arms and kisses me on the forehead. "Walk me to the door. I want to hear you lock it behind me."

"Are you going to be okay to drive?"

He holds my hand as we walk to the door. "Yeah. I never fall asleep driving."

We stop in front of the door, and he turns and cups my neck with his hands, rubbing his thumbs along my jaw.

"This does not count as one of our dates."

I place my hands on his chest. His heart thumps comfortingly beneath my palms. "Oh, really? Seemed rather date-like to me."

He tucks my hair behind my ear. "Dates are scheduled ahead of time. This doesn't count." He taps the tip of my nose with his finger. "You still owe me three more dates."

His lips capture mine, and any argument I thought to make fizzles out of my head.

CHAPTER 16

"*W*ow, this is some hill. It must be hell driving this in the winter." Kelly peers out the passenger window.

"You're probably right. I haven't been to Kerry's house before. I've missed the times she hosted book club. I think she grew up here though, so she's most likely used to it." I glance at the towering stand of pine trees on either side of the road. It's on the rural side of town —pretty.

"I'd never driven in snow before this winter. I've always lived in cities or warmer climates. If it snowed, I was using public transportation, so it didn't really affect me. It was an eye-opening experience." Kelly snickers. "There were many honking horns and finger and arm gestures done in my direction the first few times I drove in the snow."

"I bet."

"Thanks for inviting me to book club. I definitely need to get out more."

"I'm glad you could come. It's my primary indulgence these days. It's fun to hang out with the girls and chat. We discuss the books, but mostly we socialize."

"So, no men?"

"Not yet, no. Actually, I don't think anyone has ever suggested inviting men. Not even those who are blissfully in love have asked to invite their significant others."

"I imagine everyone needs a break now and then, even if they are madly in love."

The GPS on my phone speaks, "Your destination is ahead on the left."

Kelly laughs. "I really love that Irish accent. Especially when he says 'take the next right, love,' or 'three miles ahead, darlin'.' Is that a special add-on, or can I change my GPS to that too?"

"It's an add-on. I saw it on an advertisement and couldn't resist." My digital footprint must scream "single woman in need of a sexy foreign male voice."

I spot a white mailbox on the left and turn onto the gravel driveway. The sound of my tires crunching over the rocks fills the car. I slow and pray the stones won't ding my car. The driveway curves around a wooded area and then opens up into a large yard. An A-frame log cabin sits in the center.

"Isn't this pretty?"

I nod absently at Kelly. It is, but I'm too busy looking for a spot to park where my baby won't get scratched or dinged.

"Anyone I know going to be here?"

I park along the edge of the driveway in a turnaround next to the tree line. "Well, Franny and Lucinda won't be here because the wedding is only two weeks away and they're both too busy. You know Olivia, the other bridesmaid; she's supposed to be here. Then there's Sally, who works for Franny and Olivia. Barbara is Olivia's fiancé's sister-in-law. Kerry, Monica, and Tina are all teachers. Aggie is a friend of Sally's, and I think she's Monica's aunt or godmother. I'm not sure if everyone will be here, but that's the rundown."

"Was Franny the one who invited you to join?"

"Actually, no. Franny joined after I did. Monica is the founder of our little group. She and I were chatting one day when she came into my shop, and she invited me to join. It's grown over the past year. With you, we'll be almost double in size since I joined."

"You sure it's okay I came along with you?" Kelly's hand is on the door handle.

I grab my purse from the back and open my door. "Of course. The group has an open-door policy. The more the merrier." I think we're all careful who we invite. We want the group to stay fun and easygoing.

I glance up at the trees hovering over my baby. There're no dead branches in sight so she should be safe parked here.

There's a pretty stamped-concrete pathway curving along the front of the house from the driveway. The front door opens as we walk along the path.

"Hi! You made it." Kerry waves from the front steps.

I introduce them as we step inside.

"I'm so happy to meet you. I've heard wonderful things about your store and have been meaning to stop in. I'm a little afraid I'll blow my budget if I do." Kerry laughs as she shakes Kelly's hand.

"Don't worry. Not only do I have a sale rack, but I also have a payment plan for the custom-made orders."

"Ooh, did you make that?" She points to Kelly's outfit, a black pantsuit with delicate gold buttons.

"I did."

"In that case, I'll be in this week."

It's pretty cool how Kelly is often a walking advertisement for her dress shop. I suppose I could carry a bouquet of flowers or wear a corsage wherever I go, but I don't think it would have quite the same impact.

Olivia waves from the couch in the two-story living room to our left. Kelly and I wave back and she walks over to her. Kerry touches my arm before I can follow.

"I wanted to tell you before I forget. I had Drew in my class for study hall last week, and he is the sweetest, most helpful guy. Any time I asked for a volunteer for something, he would raise his hand or jump right up."

I chuckle. "He loves to help."

"His smile melts my heart." She places a hand on her chest.

"He has a brilliant smile. On the rare occasions he's feeling affectionate, he gives these giant bear hugs with a grin from ear to ear."

"Those must be very special. My brother is on the spectrum as well, and he can be stingy with his hugs."

"How old is your brother?" I didn't know she even had a brother, let alone an autistic one. I guess I'm not the only private person.

"Kyle is twenty-two. He's in this program you might find interesting for Drew. After he graduated from high school, Kyle went through the transition program where they teach them work and life skills. This other program is a continuation of that, but a little more in-depth. They're even going to help him find an apartment that suits his needs when he's ready. He still lives at home with my parents."

"That sounds amazing. I'd love to hear more about it." I wish there was an easier way to get information about benefits programs and options. It always seems to be a word-of-mouth thing. There are a few websites, but the best and most helpful information always comes from talking to other special needs families and individuals.

"I'll text you some links, and if you're interested, we can get together and talk about it. My mom would be happy to talk to you about it too. It's been a lifesaver for her. Kyle loves going and he's grown a lot."

"I'd really appreciate it."

"What does Drew do for the summer?"

"He has summer school a few mornings a week in July." Summers are one of my greatest challenges. I have to manage my store while monitoring Drew every day. Having the camera monitor helps, but it isn't the most reliable method.

"There's a camp for people with special needs. All ages are welcome. They have a nurse on staff as well as plenty of teachers and volunteers so the ratio of campers and supervision is low. The cost is negligible. They run on donations and grants. It was a game changer for my brother and my parents."

I grip Kerry's arm. "You just became one of my favorite people. Please get me the location and phone number of this heavenly place."

Kerry laughs and pats my shoulder. "I will, I promise. I'll give you my mom's information as well."

If this camp works out, it could be life-changing. A heady euphoria invades my being.

"We better go join everyone and get the meeting started. I'll text you before tomorrow."

"Please do. Otherwise, you might find me camped on your doorstep."

Kerry walks over to sit on one of the dining room chairs placed opposite the two couches perpendicular to one another facing the floor-to-ceiling windows of the A-frame. I walk toward Kelly, who is chatting with Olivia on the couch.

I wave at Sally and Aggie on the opposite couch. Monica and Tina are sitting in the other chairs with Kerry. I return their hellos and waves.

The view out the window halts me in my tracks. The sun is setting, and the horizon is lit up in peaches and pinks. Kerry's house perches on a hill with a panoramic view of one of the smaller lakes in Granite Cove. "Kerry, your view is gorgeous."

"It's what sold me on the house. I can't afford to live on the lake, so this was the next best thing for me."

"I can see why."

I sit on the other side of Kelly. "I'm sorry. I got distracted talking to Kerry. Did you get a chance to meet everyone?"

Kelly touches Olivia's arm. "Olivia introduced me."

"Great. How are you, Olivia? Ready for Franny's wedding?"

"I am. I've gotten to see and hear a lot of the plans at the bakery since Lucinda often comes downstairs to go over the details with Franny. It's going to be spectacular. I'm thinking of asking Lucinda to help plan my wedding too. You think she'd be interested?"

"It can't hurt to ask. Have you and Luke set a date?"

"We're thinking Valentine's Day. I want a winter wedding, and we got engaged on Valentine's Day so…"

"Sounds perfect."

"You could have a fur-trimmed coat or shawl to go over your wedding dress."

Olivia leans closer to Kelly. "Tell me more."

Kelly laughs. "Come into the store, and we'll brainstorm together."

"I can't wait. I didn't think I'd be one of those brides so into planning a wedding, but I'm getting slightly obsessed. Even my boys are contributing ideas for the wedding."

I lean forward and wink at Olivia. "There are a lot of choices for flowers for a winter theme too."

"I've started looking at bridal magazines. It's become a compulsion to buy one every time I go to the grocery store."

"Perfectly normal. It's an exciting time."

Olivia leans closer. "Oh, I happen to be privy to secret honeymoon news for Franny and Mitch. I also volunteered us to help pack Franny's clothes for the trip so she doesn't find out." She glances at Kelly sitting between us. "Can you keep a secret?"

Kelly mimes zipping her mouth closed.

I rest my chin on my folded hand with my elbow propped on my knee. "Franny's also clueless with clothes and couldn't care less about fashion."

Olivia winces. "Not sure I'd put it quite that way."

"That's because you're too sweet, but Franny would be the first to admit she doesn't care about clothes."

"True, she would."

"So, where are they going?"

Olivia glances around the room and whispers, "Mitch has arranged for a private yacht on the Mediterranean Sea. He's also given me carte blanche to buy whatever is necessary to supplement her wardrobe for the trip."

"That sounds divine. He's a keeper."

Kelly soundlessly nods between us.

"We'll have to plan to get a look at her closet beforehand. A reconnaissance trip so we can make a list of what she needs—with her unaware, of course."

"I can help with that."

Olivia and I both look at Kelly.

"Franny is coming in to look at some shawl options on Monday morning in case the weather doesn't warm up for the wedding."

The temperature has been hovering in the sixties. It could be a little chilly for the outdoor wedding.

I nod. Both The Sweet Spot and Blossoms are closed on Mondays. "That sounds like a good opportunity." I look at Olivia. "Does that work for you?"

"Yes. I'll clear it with Mitch and make sure we can get into the house."

"We have a plan."

Kelly laughs. "You sound like spies planning an intelligence mission or something."

Olivia shakes her head. "I'd make a terrible spy. I don't have a poker face. Everything I'm thinking is written on my face." She points a short pink fingernail at me. "You, on the other hand, would make a great spy. You're so cool and collected. No one knows what you're thinking or feeling unless you tell them."

I smirk. "It's called resting bitch face."

CHAPTER 17

"What am I going to eat? They don't have my food." Drew shoves the menu away from him and knocks over the salt and pepper shakers in the middle of the table.

The woman behind Drew swivels around and stares. I stare right back until she turns back to her own plate.

I set the salt and pepper upright. "Drew, take a breath. We'll find you something to eat. You haven't even looked at the menu yet. I know this restaurant is new to you, but they have tasty food here too." *Please let them have something he'll eat.*

"Do you want to go somewhere else?"

I force a smile to my lips and glance over at Ian sitting next to me. "No, this is fine. Drew gets anxious over change." I look at Drew. "But he will remember his manners and apologize for his outburst while I look at the menu and find him something he can and will eat. Right, Drew?"

He glances at Ian, shrugs, and mumbles at the table, "Sorry."

Curling my toes in the tips of my shoes, I open and scan the menu. The evening has barely begun, and my blood pressure is already spiking. When Ian called and invited me out to dinner, I declined. Then he reminded me of the bet and the dates I owed him. I told him my babysitter was unavailable, thinking that would be the end of it, and he invited Drew to come along.

What was I thinking by accepting?

"What do you like to eat?" Ian peers over his menu and smiles at Drew.

Drew shrugs and gazes around the restaurant.

"Drew has been gluten-free for years. He's not allergic, but with his autism and ADHD, it helps with his behavior. Not sure what it is about his brain chemistry, but gluten is a bit like a drug to him. He gets super hyper and irritable. He craves it, too, to the point where there was a time it was all he wanted to eat."

"I'll check with the waitress to see what they have that's gluten-free. If they have nothing he likes, we can go somewhere that does." Ian stood and strode toward the hostess stand at the front of the restaurant.

"How about a burger without a bun? You love cheeseburgers. They have steak too. You could have a baked potato. Oh, look, they have sweet potatoes too."

Drew meets my gaze. "Sweet potato?"

"Yup, you want one?"

"Can they put butter and cinnamon on it like you do?"

"I'm sure that won't be a problem."

"Okay."

"What do you want with it? Burger or steak?"

"Burger. No lettuce or tomato."

Ian returns with a small piece of paper. "This is what she gave me. There aren't many options. Why don't we find a restaurant more accommodating?" He stands with his hands on the back of the chair.

"It's fine. Drew is going to have a burger without a bun and a baked sweet potato. I'm sorry for the fuss."

"There's no fuss." He glances between me and Drew. "Are you sure you want to stay?"

"I like sweet potatoes."

Ian smiles. "So do I." He takes his seat as the waitress arrives and takes all our orders.

I sigh and lean back in my chair. The wooden chair creaks and the top pokes into my shoulder blades. I shift and cross my legs. I flick a piece of lint off my black pants and tap the heel of my black shoes against my foot.

There's a cowboy theme in the steakhouse. A painting of cantering horses hangs over the wall across from us. A saddle acts as a divider between sections of the room.

"I know you like cars, but what else do you like, Drew?"

"Uh, I don't know." He shrugs and grins.

"You like animals."

He nods and looks at Ian. "Can we go back to your farm? I like the animals there."

"That was Ian's moms' farm."

"I'm sure they would love to have you come over any time."

I try not to wince. Drew will interpret that as an engraved invitation, and I won't hear the end of it until we go. He's very literal and tenacious.

"I like fishing too."

Ugh, I dropped the ball on that one. Planning a fishing outing was more complicated than I'd thought. You need a fishing license, equipment, and the time and inclination. I temporarily placated him with a trip to the town beach with a net and a bucket. He had fun tromping through the water looking for whatever creatures he could find, but he still asked about fishing.

"I know I still owe you a fishing trip."

"You like to fish?" Ian gazed at me with a surprised smile on his face.

"No, but Drew does, and his school trip got canceled, so I promised to take him."

Ian turns to Drew. "I enjoy fishing too. My brothers and I used to go all the time. My brother Mike owns a fishing boat. I bet he'd let me borrow it." He glances back to me with a raised eyebrow.

Drew practically bounces in his chair. "Can we?"

"That's very nice of you, Ian." It would fulfill my promise, and it would help to have someone who actually knows what they're doing along. I don't relish the thought of touching gross wiggling worms or slimy fish. "If you're sure you don't mind, that would be great."

"I don't mind at all. In fact, I'm looking forward to it. It's been a while since I went fishing."

"It would have to be after I close the shop."

"We can do that, or we could go before you open. The fishing is best in the early morning."

I glance at him sideways. "How early?"

"Dawn."

God, help me.

"Sissy doesn't like mornings."

"She doesn't, huh?"

Drew shakes his head and grins. "She has alarms, and when they go off, she swears a lot."

I'm not even looking at Ian, but I can feel his smirk. I give Drew a mock glare. "Drew, you aren't supposed to tattle on me."

He giggles. "You do though…a lot."

"Okay, I've never been a morning person, and I don't swear every morning." At least not loud enough he can hear me across the hall.

"We can go later, if you prefer."

"I can get up early." I'll put the alarm clock on the other side of the room so I have to get out of bed to shut it off like I do when my phone alarm goes off. It only takes hitting the snooze button a couple of times to get me out of bed. It's not like I sleep through them and don't get up at all.

"Great! How about tomorrow, then?"

"Tomorrow? Don't you have to call your brother and make sure it's okay?"

"I'm sure it will be, and if not, I've got a couple of friends who have boats who owe me favors."

How nice for him. I muster up some enthusiasm and smile at them, both grinning at each other like they just won the lottery or something.

I look forward to sleeping in an extra couple of hours on Saturdays. I don't have to get up to get Drew ready for school on the week-ends. It looks like I'll have to forgo my beauty sleep tomorrow and next week, too, since it's Franny's wedding.

"I'll program the coffee maker to turn on at dawn."

"We want to be out on the water at sunrise, so you might want to program it a little earlier. And make sure you bring a jacket. It gets chilly on the water this early in the spring."

"Wonderful."

Ian chuckles while Drew claps. His excitement shines like he's harnessed his own tiny sun.

The waitress delivers Drew's burger and sweet potato, Ian's prime rib with sweet potato, and my filet mignon, mashed potatoes, and broccoli. It's been at least a year since I had a steak. Drew and I stick to takeout when I don't muster up the energy to cook. Joe's Pizzeria makes a terrific gluten-free pizza Drew scarfs down all on his own. When I give in to his pleading to eat out, that's always his first choice. He sticks with his favorites. He's not one to branch out and experiment.

I reach over and cut up Drew's burger and sweet potato. "There you go."

"Thanks, Sissy."

"You're welcome."

I see Ian glance over at Drew's plate while he cuts into his own sweet potato and adds the butter.

"Drew has dyspraxia. Coordination skills, especially the fine motor ones, are a challenge for him."

Ian nods and then winks at Drew. "My mother used to cut my brother Ryan's meat for him well into his twenties, and he didn't have a diagnosis."

Drew grins. "I do. I have lots of them."

Ian laughs, and I shake my head, smiling.

"Are you going to eat the fish we catch tomorrow?"

"I like fish."

Ian leans his head closer to mine. "Are you going to cook the fish for us?"

I wrinkle my nose. I hate the smell of cooking fish, but if he's willing to take Drew fishing, the least I can do is cook it.

"Confident in your fishing skills, are you? What if you don't catch any?"

"We're men. Of course we're going to catch fish. Right, Drew?"

Drew nods emphatically and giggles.

I roll my eyes but refrain from commenting on his gender-biased boast.

"Besides, if we get desperate, I can call my mom."

"Your mother likes fishing?"

"Not really, but whenever she went with us and we weren't catching anything she would put down whatever book she was reading, lean real close to the water, and whisper, 'Fishy, fishy, fishy.'" He cuts a piece of his prime rib. "Worked like a charm every time."

"I believe it. I think your mother is gifted. She has a magical quality about her."

He takes a sip of his water and smiles at me like he just figured out the meaning of life or something.

"What?"

"You like my mother."

"Of course I like your mother. She's very kind and genuine. Why do you sound surprised?"

"I'm not surprised. It just occurred to me I probably have my mother to thank for you finally agreeing to go out with me. Did you decide I couldn't be so bad if I share her DNA?"

"Maybe. Of course, your twin brother got all the looks, so maybe he got her kindness too. What do you say you introduce us sometime? You said he moved back to New Hampshire, right?"

Ian scowls and slices off a piece of meat before chomping it off his fork.

I turn my head to hide the smile I can't hold back. He's touchy about his brother. He makes it too easy to push his buttons.

"Drew, use your napkin, not your shirt."

He stops wiping his fingers on his shirt and picks up his napkin.

Ian clasps my wrist, which is resting on the table, lifts it to his lips, and presses a lingering kiss against the underside.

He leans over, tucks my hair behind my ear, and whispers, "You think my brother will make your pulse jump with a single touch or know how sensitive your skin is right here?" His fingers drift over the back of my neck as his breath caresses right below my ear.

A shiver ripples over my skin.

He chuckles and kisses me behind my ear and leans back in his seat. I slowly lift my napkin and dab at my lips before dropping it next to my plate.

The man certainly gets my engine revving, and he knows it too. I glance at my brother, who is happily chewing on the remainder of his sweet potato. He's not paying us the slightest bit of attention.

I glance discreetly over my shoulder. We're against the wall, so no one is behind us. There's only one table next to Ian, and the man's back faces us. I slip my hand from my lap and over to Ian's.

He freezes with his fork in the air. His gaze swings to mine.

I squeeze his thigh right next to his groin.

His eyes widen, and his hand drops to the table. There's a telltale swelling against the side of my hand.

I lick my lips. His gaze tracks the motion. There's a slight flush to the skin over his cheekbones.

I may not be immune to his touch, but he's not immune to mine either.

His Adam's apple bobs as he swallows.

My fingers brush against his erection as I release them one by one. I remove my hand from his lap and brush my hair back before picking up my glass and taking a long sip of water.

Ian scoots his chair over to mine and lays his arm over the back of my chair. His head is right next to mine.

I slowly turn my head and meet his gaze.

He looks hungry—and not for food.

I purse my lips. "It's a shame we have to get up so early. We'll have to get to bed early tonight."

One eyebrow lifts. I can guess what he's thinking. He's wondering if I'm about to break my rule and invite him to my bed with Drew home.

Drew chugs down the rest of his soda. "I'm done."

"It's a good thing we took separate cars. That way Ian can go straight home and go to bed, and we can do the same."

Ian whispers under his breath. "You're a heartless tease, killer. I see a long, cold shower in my future."

I flutter my eyelashes at him. "You did say it would be chilly on the lake in the morning. I bet the lake would be downright frigid. You can go for a swim."

One eyebrow lifts. "Are you less than subtly telling me to go jump in the lake?"

I smirk. "Now when have I ever been subtle about telling you where to go?"

CHAPTER 18

The coffee maker gurgles. We lost power sometime last night, so not only did my backup alarm not go off, but my coffee maker didn't have my coffee waiting for me.

Drew is happily chattering away, sitting at the breakfast bar behind me, eating his second bowl of cereal. I turn the cup on the coffee platform. It's a picture of a younger Drew grinning and holding a frog. I smile and shake my head. That kid is a fountain of joy over the simplest things.

I laid out a pair of jeans, long-sleeved shirt, and a hoodie for him last night. He's already dressed and ready to go.

I pull the coffee cup out from under the coffee maker while it's still dripping and splash in a healthy amount of creamer and sugar. I'll worry about the calories later. I need this.

I plod out of the kitchen with the cup cradled in my hands. The outside steps creak under someone's weight. I close my eyes.

He's early. I glance down at my white silk pajamas and then up at the ceiling. How am I going to make it through this day?

I take a deep swallow of the hot coffee. With lots and lots of coffee.

He knocks on the door. I walk over and peek through the hole to verify it's Ian. Yup, it's him with a baseball cap advertising his bar on his head.

Sighing, I walk back over to the kitchen. "Let Ian in. I'm going to go get dressed."

"Okay!" Drew jumps up from the stool and runs to the front door.

I skirt around him and stride down the hallway to my bedroom.

Less than ten minutes later, I walk into the living room to find Ian playing cars with Drew on the floor.

"Morning, beautiful." He stands with a smile.

I know I don't look my best, but warmth spreads through me at his words anyway. I did little more than comb my hair and brush my teeth after tugging on a pair of jeans and a sweatshirt.

He's got a scruff of a beard darkening his jaw I find oddly adorable. I've always preferred a clean-shaven man. I've never seen him with any facial hair before. Maybe I'm not the only one who had a rough time waking up this morning.

"Mike is meeting us at the boat ramp near the docks. I've got my Jeep with all the fishing gear parked right outside your door."

"One perk of being up so early. You don't need to worry about parking. Nothing is open this early."

"The Sweet Spot is." He jerks his head to the bar.

A pair of familiar black and pink coffee cups sits in the middle. My mouth opens and closes. "I could kiss you right now." I stride over to the bar.

"I won't object. The one on the left is yours."

I snatch it up and pop open the top of the lid and take a whiff. He remembered my favorite. I blow into the lid and take a hesitant sip. Perfect. I drink half the cup before closing my eyes and sighing.

Ian stands next to me when I open my eyes.

"You really do love your coffee." He taps his lips. "I believe you owe me a kiss."

I glance at Drew and then lean up and plant a noisy kiss on Ian's cheek. "Thank you."

"You're welcome. Drew, the other cup is a hot chocolate for you."

He glances at Drew. "You like hot chocolate, right? Franny assured me it's gluten-free."

I smile behind the lid of my cup as I take a sip. Drew nods and jumps up.

"All ready to go?" Ian hands Drew the cup and looks at me.

I nod. As ready as I'll ever be.

Drew rattles off a bunch of questions about Ian's Jeep as we climb in and drive out of the parking lot. He chatters the entire short drive across the street and down to the town boat ramp while Ian answers all his questions.

The lights cast a golden glow over the parking lot. Mike stands next to a truck with a boat and a trailer attached. Ian waves as he pulls into a parking space. Remarkably, the small lot is already quite full of empty trailers. I guess we're not the earliest people out here this morning.

Mike strolls over and greets Ian with a pat on the back as he climbs out of the Jeep.

"You remember Drew and Rebecca from Mom's party?" Ian holds the seat forward for Drew to climb out while I exit my side.

I wave through the open doors of the Jeep. Mike lifts a hand in return and smiles, then gives Drew a fist bump.

"How's it going? Ready to catch some fish this morning?"

"Yes!" Drew grins from ear to ear.

I sip at the rest of my coffee, wishing it would automatically refill itself, while they unload rods and tackle boxes from the vehicles and put them in the boat. Mike gets in the truck and backs the boat down the ramp into the water.

There's barely a ripple along the surface of the water. The sun peeks through the trees across the cove. A gray haze hovers over the lake. It is peaceful this time of the morning.

Mike drives the truck back up the ramp and parks it and the trailer by the opening to the lot. Ian stands next to the boat, holding a rope. He's talking to Drew. I wander closer.

"Think you can swing your leg over and climb in?"

I look from Ian to the boat and then at Drew. This could go wrong in so many ways. I quicken my pace until I stop behind the two of them.

Drew stares hard at the boat. I know how badly he wants this, and I don't want him disappointed.

"How about we wait for Mike? He can hold the back of the boat over there while I hold on to the front. That way it will be steadier, okay?"

Drew nods silently.

I glance at Ian.

"I should have thought to have him in the boat before it went into the water. If this doesn't work, we can bring it over to the docks and he can climb in there."

"Okay."

Mike walks down, and he and Ian discuss the best way to help Drew into the boat. Mike is a couple inches shorter than Ian and beefier. He has the same dark hair and tan skin. It's obvious they're related, but his blue eyes are lighter and his features, sharper.

"You want to get in here or over at the docks, buddy?"

Drew chews on his lip as he stares at Mike. "Here."

"Okay, then let's do it."

I hold my breath while they hold the boat as steady as they can. The boat is practically on shore before they prompt Drew to climb on. I put my coffee on the ground and get behind him in case he falls. He'll squash me like a bug if he does, but I can't stand here and do nothing.

Drew lands on his knees inside the boat, but he's in. He stands with a grin. We all cheer for him, and I clap my hands.

I pick up my coffee and take a drink. Wait, I need to climb into the boat too.

This will not be graceful. I look around for a garbage can for my empty cup as I swallow the last of it.

Ian swings me up into his arms, and I choke as I grasp for his shoulders. My coffee cup goes flying and bounces off the pavement. He grins at me and walks over to the boat.

"Don't you dare drop me."

He changes direction and walks to the edge of the lake.

"What are you doing?!" I clutch his shoulders and stare at the water.

"I seem to remember a reference to jumping in the lake."

Mike holds the front of the boat with one hand and rubs his smiling face with the other. Drew sits in the high seat in the middle of the boat, inspecting one of the tackle boxes. No help from either of them.

I glare at Ian. "If you drop me in the lake, I promise you I will have my revenge, and it will be much, much worse."

"I have no doubt of that, sweetheart. I'm not going to drop you in the lake. For a price, of course."

"Blackmail?"

"Depends how you look at it, I suppose."

"What's the price?"

He stares into my eyes. "Nothing too steep. Just a kiss—on the lips."

I glance over to the boat. Drew is still busy digging through the tackle box. Mike is looking everywhere but at us and scratching the back of his neck.

"One."

He leans his head down. "Help me out here, beautiful. My hands are kind of busy." He shifts his hold on me.

I let out an embarrassing squeak and wrap my arms around his neck. He chuckles and lifts me higher and captures my lips with his.

I intended for the kiss to be brief, but clearly Ian has other ideas. His tongue sweeps inside my mouth and before I know it, I'm kissing him back.

A whistle sounds behind us, and I tear my mouth away from his. Ian scowls at his brother while Mike snickers back at him.

"Thought we were going fishing, little brother?"

Ian carries me over to the boat and swings me over the side. My feet touch the bottom, and his hands linger on my body, sliding over me, as I stand.

He swipes my coffee cup off the ground and pitches it into the garbage can effortlessly and then vaults over the side of the boat. Mike does the same after tossing the rope into the front of the boat.

Mike walks past me to the back of the boat while Ian sits in the front seat, looks at me, and pats his lap.

"Not in this lifetime," I mutter and look around for a place to sit. There are only the three seats. Am I supposed to sit on the floor? I frown and try to decide the best place to plop down.

Mike starts the engine, then flips up a seat next to him. He pats the cushion and winks at me.

"Switch with me, Mike." Ian stands.

Mike grins and shakes his head slowly. "No one drives my boat but me."

Ian plants his fists on his hips. "Seriously?"

Mike chuckles. "Afraid I'm going to steal your lady, little brother?"

I roll my eyes and drop onto the seat. The brothers had teased each other mercilessly at the picnic too. "It's much too early in the morning for these theatrics."

CHAPTER 19

"Trying to spot celebrities?" Olivia leans over my shoulder and peeks out the second-story window of Mitch and Franny's house. Guests have been arriving steadily, and the chairs arranged in rows on the back lawn are filling up. Only a half hour or so until the wedding ceremony is scheduled to begin.

"No, I'm checking on Drew." Franny insisted on inviting him to her wedding, and when I broached the subject with him, he seemed excited. As a bridesmaid, I can't be with him for the ceremony, so I had planned for a sitter, but I couldn't disappoint him.

"He looks happy between Ian and Kerry." She turns her head to face me. "Things appear to be heating up between you and Ian."

"He won a few dates from me in a bet. One of them turned into a fishing excursion with Drew last week, and when my brother learned Ian was going to the wedding, too, he immediately asked to sit together. Ian agreed instantly. I had already asked Kerry if she wouldn't mind keeping an eye on him while I was busy with bridesmaid duties. He knows her from school." I'd asked Kelly to watch out for him, too, and thought he'd sit between them, but he knows Ian more, so it's not surprising he wanted to sit next to him. Kelly sits on

Kerry's other side. The rest of the book club members are spread out around them.

"I know it's nerve-racking worrying about him, but there are plenty of people down there looking out for him."

She's right. All the book club members will keep an eye on him too.

Olivia texts on her phone and then looks up. "There. Luke will keep an eye out too."

I spot him and her twin boys two rows behind Drew. "Don't you think he has his hands full watching your sons? Not that I don't appreciate the extra support."

She chuckles. "Luke is surprisingly adept at keeping them in line, and Barbara is there too."

"How are things with your future sister-in-law?"

"She's fantastic and so great with the boys. They already call her Aunt Barbara, and her little Joey calls me Auntie Liv. I love it."

I wrap my arm around her shoulders and give her a quick squeeze. "I'm really happy for you."

"Me too." She laughs and puts her arm around my waist. "I like Ian. I admit I don't know him all that well—only as an acquaintance—but he's always kind, and I've never heard a negative word about him."

"I like him, too, but I'm not looking for a relationship."

"What are you two whispering about over here? Aren't the brides-maids supposed to be doting on the bride on her wedding day?" Franny props her chin on my shoulder and grins between us.

We laugh and turn to face her. "Absolutely. Please tell us how we may serve you, dear bride." Olivia curtsies.

I mimic her curtsy. These formal blue gowns seem to call for royal treatment. They're not something I want to wear regularly, but they are exquisite. Kelly outdid herself. "Shall we tell you again how gorgeous you are? How you radiate love from your every pore and your eyes shine with joy?"

Franny throws back her head and laughs. "Oh, you know I'm joking, but I am so happy. Because I'm marrying the love of my life, of course, but also because I have all the people I love around me on this special day." She puts her arms around us for a group hug.

"Hey, I want a piece of this!" Lucinda ducks under Franny's arm to join in. She lays her head on Franny's shoulder. "Oh, dang it! Here come the tears again. I don't know why I bothered with makeup today."

Franny laughs. "Luce, you have turned into a watering pot today. I thought I would be the one crying on my wedding day."

"I know, but I'm just so happy for you."

"Well, before this turns into a crying fest and ruins all our makeup and the poor makeup artists have to come back in and fix us, we should have a toast to Franny on her wedding day."

"You're absolutely right, Olivia." Lucinda walks over to the small round table where a bottle of champagne sits in a silver ice bucket with four champagne glasses in front of it. She pours each of us a glass and hands them to us. "To Franny, my wonderful baby sister. I'm so happy for you and so proud. And I'm going to leave it at that for now because the tears are starting again. I love you."

Franny kisses Lucinda's cheek. "I love you, too, and thank you again for planning my fairy tale wedding better than I ever dreamed."

Olivia raises her glass. "I second that and add my plea to help plan my wedding."

Lucinda gives her a watery smile. "I'll be happy to help."

Olivia places her hand over her chest. "Okay, no tears." She clears her throat. "Franny, you're not only my business partner." She shakes her head. "Gosh, I love saying that. You're my best friend. You've given me so much. I'm so thrilled to be sharing this day with you. Here's to a lifetime of wonderful days ahead for you and Mitch."

Franny and Olivia hug and rock back and forth.

"So much for no more tears. We've all turned into leaky faucets." I raise my glass. "Franny, I'm so honored to be here today. You've shown me what genuine friendship can mean. I love all of you, and I'm so happy I moved to Granite Cove and met all of you."

Franny hugs me and turns with a sniffle. "You all know I don't drink much—and I really hope this one glass of champagne doesn't go to my head and have me tripping down the aisle—but it's so worth it because I love you all so much. I can't believe how much my life has changed in a year, and it's due in a large part to all of you. Thank you from the bottom of my heart."

"Now we really do need touchups. Let's get this done before Mother comes back and loses her mind over our dishevelment." Lucinda sashays over to the full-length mirror and peers at her face.

"Where is Mother?" Franny frowns and looks around the room.

"She's happiest when she's telling people what to do, so I had her go check on the caterers. That way she wouldn't start managing us." Lucinda walks to the door. "I'm going to ask the makeup artists to come in for a finishing touchup. It's almost time for us to go downstairs."

I look out the window for a last check while Franny and Olivia walk over to the dressing area. Drew's head tilts to the side, and I can see him laughing at something Ian is saying. He's fine—better than fine. He's happy. I smile and let my gaze drift over the lawn. My flower arrangements are all in place. The enormous bouquets in tall vases stand ready for the ceremony in the white gazebo down by the lake. The chairs are all lined up before the gazebo and full of guests. The giant tent for the reception is set up on the side lawn. The string quartet plays an uplifting melody as the last attendees take their seats.

The sun is shining and there isn't a cloud in sight. The day couldn't be more magical for Franny's wedding day.

THE SUN DISAPPEARS below the horizon, leaving the spectacular pinks and golds of the sunset to slowly fade away. Drew plays with Olivia's twins and another boy in the low maze of bushes landscaped on the side of the house. Who would have thought my brother would be playing with Holden Fox's son? I guess it's not so surprising a famous actor would be Mitch's best man.

"I finally find you alone." Ian hands me a glass of champagne and wraps his arm around my shoulders.

I glance over my shoulder at the reception still going strong in the tent on the other side of the house. Every facet of the wedding and reception had been perfect. Lucinda outdid herself. Franny and Mitch both haven't stopped smiling all day.

"Except for the sendoff on their honeymoon, I believe my brides-maid duties are about over. Thank you again for watching Drew." Franny's luggage is packed with exquisite clothing, much of it from Kelly's store. Olivia and I had so much fun purchasing a new wardrobe for Franny's honeymoon.

"Stop thanking me. I enjoy hanging out with him. Besides, he's been with those three for most of it." He points to the boys as they race along the maze, playing whatever imagined game they dreamed up. They're all several years younger and smaller than Drew, but none of them seem to notice.

I glance over to where Olivia and Luke sit on a stone bench, watching the boys play. I should talk to her about setting up a play-date. Drew doesn't have many friends. It's one of the main reasons I'm so looking forward to the summer camp I signed him up for. He needs friends to run around and laugh with.

"Have I told you how beautiful you look in that dress? It's given me quite a few fantasies."

"Would you like to have the dress? I'm done with it after tonight."

"Hilarious. It's not the dress I want, but the woman wearing it."

"Let me guess—the fantasies involve subservient women beholden to men for every aspect of their lives?"

"If I wanted a subservient woman, I wouldn't be chasing after you."

I gaze at his handsome face. A lock of his dark hair hangs over his forehead. My fingers itch to brush it back, but that would be too inti-mate—something a girlfriend would do. I can't go there.

"What *do* you want, Ian? I told you I don't do relationships."

"I remember. Am I pushing you into anything? I don't recall trying to label us or asking you for a commitment." He removes his arm from my shoulder and puts his hands in his pants pockets.

"No, you haven't. I just want us to be clear where we both stand so there're no misconceptions or hurt feelings."

"Okay, friends with benefits. Does that about cover it?"

It's exactly what I wanted so why does it sound sordid? "I suppose so."

"There is one little detail I want to clear up."

"What's that?"

"While you're sleeping with me, you aren't sleeping with anyone else."

"Does that go both ways?"

Ian grips the sides of my waist. "I haven't had the slightest interest in another woman since a gorgeous one snuck out of my hotel room in the middle of the night."

No other women? His image as a player might need revising—if he's telling the truth.

I spread my hands over his chest. "Do a lot of women sneak out on you? You might want to check into that." I pat his bicep.

He shakes his head and lowers his mouth to hover over mine. "Vixen. Why did you run?"

I raise my gaze from his lips, inches from mine, to his sea-blue eyes. "You scared the hell out of me with all your personal questions and talk of meeting again."

"You're still running scared, aren't you?"

"I'm not running anywhere. As long as we're clear on the boundaries, this can be enjoyable for both of us."

"Enjoyment has not been a problem for us from the start." His mouth captures mine in a passionate kiss that leaves me forgetting for a moment where we are and who could be watching.

I step out of his arms and look around. No one appears to be paying us any attention. Drew is still happily playing beneath the strings of lights casting a glow over the garden landscape. Olivia and Luke are lost in an embrace of their own.

"I don't think it's a good idea for public displays. It will only cause awkward questions, and I don't want Drew to get the wrong idea."

"What wrong idea?"

"He's already lost so much in his young life. I don't want him to get attached to you."

"Regardless of what happens between you and me, I intend to stay in Drew's life. I consider him a friend. But I can respect your wishes and keep the kisses for when we're alone."

"Thank you." I drop my gaze. He wants to stay in Drew's life? That could be beneficial for Drew if he means it. Drew needs more positive role models. Not sure how I feel about it for me though.

"Speaking of alone, you still owe me some dates. What about Monday? It's your day off. You can come to my house for lunch."

I sigh. "Fine."

"Your excitement is overwhelming."

CHAPTER 20

hat was I thinking by admitting I ran because I was scared? It must have been the champagne. Honesty is not always the best policy.

Mom would be so disappointed to hear me say that or think that. She was the most honest person ever. Sometimes too honest—like when she told me my prom date was not good enough for me and would never love me more than he loved himself. She was right, of course. I didn't believe her at the time and was mad as hell with her.

I miss her. I miss talking to her about my life and hearing her advice—even if I don't always want to take it. I miss her smile and her hugs. I miss Dad's laughter. He always had a corny dad joke to share.

Drew mentioned fishing with Dad a couple of times on our outing with Ian. I had forgotten they used to go fishing together. What else had I forgotten?

Was I not talking about our parents enough with Drew? Sometimes the days are so busy and overwhelming it's all I can do just to get through them, but I want to keep their memories alive for him... for both of us.

The GPS announces my destination ahead on the left. I search for Ian's mailbox number. My fingers tap against the steering wheel. It's just lunch. A debt owed. We've been forthcoming with each other about our arrangement. We're both on the same page. Nothing to worry about.

A simple black metal mailbox marks the end of his driveway. I make the turn and say a little thanks for the paved driveway. I don't want any dings in my car. Towering evergreens line the driveway and fill the woods in both directions. Instead of grass, pine needles cover the ground. It's like driving into an enchanted forest.

I step on the brake as the house comes into view. A modern design of dark wooden angles and glass perches in the middle of a manicured lawn with clumps of white birch trees. I park in front of the two-car garage next to the stone pathway to the front door. The wide wooden door opens as I step out of my car.

Ian walks out dressed in a pair of jeans and a light gray T-shirt. He jogs down the stairs and walkway barefoot.

"You made it." He cups my cheeks in his hands and kisses me.

"I did. This is amazing. How long have you lived here?"

"I bought the property almost two years ago and had Mike design the house."

"Mike? Your brother?"

"Yeah, he's an architect."

"I didn't know that."

"He's also my neighbor. He bought the lot next to mine."

I turn my head in both directions, but I can't see any sign of another house.

Ian chuckles. "You can't see it from here. If we walk down the backyard path that leads to the beach, you can catch a glimpse of it."

"Beach?"

"It belongs to the association. All the houses here are part of it. I don't have waterfront property, but I get some of the advantages without the price tag or tax bill. We can take a walk down there if you want."

"I'd like to see it, but first I want to see your house."

He waves a hand for me to precede him down the walk. There are a variety of bushes lining the side of the walkway next to the house.

Spiral towers and round cushions of varying shades of green with smooth stones covering the ground.

"Who does your landscaping? It's beautiful."

"Local guy, Bob Calvert. Went to school together, but he was a few years behind me."

The front door is twice the size of a regular door and looks like it weighs a ton, but it swings open effortlessly and soundlessly.

I gasp as I walk inside. There's an open expanse encompassing a living room, kitchen, and eating area. Soaring ceilings with wooden beams and glass-filled walls frame the space. "Wow!"

"You like it?"

"I love it." I slip out of my shoes and leave them by the closet on the right of the door. "What's the floor made of?" It's smooth as glass but solid with a swirl pattern of shades of gray.

"Concrete."

"Really? It looks too shiny to be concrete." I step from the stones of the entryway onto the cement. The surface is as smooth as tile, not rough like a sidewalk.

"It's polished and sealed."

"It's warm not cold."

"Heated floors."

"That must be bliss in the winter."

There's a giant island separating the kitchen and living room. It's longer than the width of my bedroom. Stainless steel appliances and white counters balance the wooden open shelves. A massive sectional couch occupies half the living space while a pool table is centered on the other half.

"This really is spectacular, Ian. Your brother is a talented architect."

"Yeah, he is, but we try not to let him get too much of a swelled head." Ian runs his hand down my back and rests it over my hip.

"Do you want to see the rest or eat lunch first?"

"I want to see the rest first, but what's for lunch?"

"Grilled salmon, risotto, and a honey fig salad."

I turn away from peering down the hallway and open set of stairs on the right. "Where did you pick up that?"

"I didn't. I cook. If you came into my pub occasionally, you'd know I set the menu and occasionally help in the kitchen. My brother isn't the only one with talents."

"I was avoiding you, but now that I don't have to do that anymore, I will."

"Glad to hear it." He takes my hand and draws me down the hallway. The open set of stairs leads up and down.

"That door leads to the garage." He points to the door at the end of the hallway. "This is the main bathroom." He gestures to the open door next to us. It's a full bathroom with a large walk-in shower, a separate tub, and a double sink vanity. The tile is in shades of blue like the ocean.

"That's the laundry room." He points to a door perpendicular to the door to the garage. "And these two across from one another are bedrooms. Only that one has a bed currently. Mike crashed here until his place was finished. The master is upstairs."

I get only a vague impression of large rooms with scarce furniture before he tugs me upstairs. There's a small landing to the right and then a set of double doors open to reveal a bedroom larger than my entire apartment. The furniture is scarce in here, too, except for the massive bed in the center against the far wall. A walk-in closet and a bathroom occupy the right side of the space.

All I see is white when he points to the bathroom, so I step closer and peer inside. A circular gray tub dominates the room. There's a giant walk-in shower along with a double sink vanity, but all I can stare at is the tub.

"That's practically a swimming pool."

He chuckles and leans an arm on the doorjamb over my head. "Not really."

"You must really like baths."

"I admit I've only used it a few times. I saw it in a magazine once and thought it was cool, so I had Mike design the bathroom around it."

"It makes one hell of a statement. I'd live in it if I had that tub."

"Feel free to use it any time."

I give him a sideways look. "Careful what you offer. For that tub, I could make myself a pest."

"That I would like to see."

"What's out there?" I gesture with my chin to the sliding doors across from us.

"A balcony. I had Mike add a set of stairs down to the deck so I could go straight to the pool and jump in without walking through the whole house."

"There's a pool?" I wander over to the doors, slide them open, and step out onto the balcony. The pool is kidney-shaped with a hot tub on one end.

"I like to swim, and the lake is cold more often than not. The pool is heated so I can go for a swim any time I want. I've been known to keep it open until after the first snowfall."

I glance at him over my shoulder. "Snow?"

"Yeah, it's magical swimming in the pool or relaxing in the hot tub when the snow is falling all around you."

"I'll take your word for it."

"You need to try it at least once. I'd be tempted to keep it open year-round, but the heating bills can be killer."

"I bet." I turn and face him, leaning against the railing. "I can't stop thinking about that meal you promised me."

"Good. Let's go downstairs and feed you."

As we descend, I point to the lower staircase. "What's down there?"

"Right now, mostly open space. I haven't decided what to do with it yet. There's a utility room and a rough bathroom, but the rest is all open. I have my workout equipment scattered around."

We walk into the kitchen, where he pulls out a stool at the end of the island.

"Now sit and let me dazzle you with my culinary abilities."

I slide on to the stool with a smile. "Dazzle away. I'll sit right here and watch you labor over our meal."

He leans one hand on the island, cups my jaw with the other, and kisses me. "For inspiration," he whispers.

He pours a glass of wine and hands it to me.

I prop my chin on my hand and watch as he pulls ingredients out of the fridge and prepares our lunch. I'm a decent cook, but he looks like an actual chef as he wields a knife across a cutting board and moves between the stove and counter.

"Your salad, milady."

He sets a plate with mixed greens and figs drizzled in honey in front of me and an identical plate before himself.

I pause with the first bite in my mouth. It's the perfect combination of tangy and sweet. I glance at him and cover my mouth while I finish chewing. "This is unbelievable. Consider me impressed. Feel free to cook for me any time."

The rest of the meal is just as delicious. He pulls out a box from The Sweet Spot for dessert, and I shake my head.

"As much as I love sweets and Franny's are the best, I couldn't eat another bite. Besides, that risotto was decadence itself."

He winks and sets the box down. "Then mission accomplished. The sweets will hold until later."

"Later?"

He takes my hands and pulls me off the stool.

"You still have a couple of hours until Drew gets home from school, right?"

"Yes."

"Then I think it's time for you to take a closer look at my bed." He wraps his arms around my waist and folds them together behind my back.

"Oh? And what's so special about your bed? It looked pretty average."

"Average? Not even close, sweetheart. It's a California king and adjustable to fit any level of comfort you desire."

"Special tub, special bed... You are spoiled, aren't you?"

"I only want the best, beautiful." He kisses my forehead, the tip of my nose, and then my lips. He lingers against my mouth while I slide my hands over his chest and shoulders to loop my arms around his neck.

"Show me this wonderful bed."

CHAPTER 21

*I*an's warm hand engulfs mine as I follow him up the stairs. I can't help but stare at his backside as it flexes with each step. What type of workout equipment does he have in the basement? I've seen his body on a couple of occasions now, and there isn't any room for improvement. His muscles are etched and defined. I bet artists would go nuts for a chance to draw him or sculpt him in clay. If I had to guess, I'd say there were weight machines. Maybe a treadmill, too, because he certainly has endurance. Though that could be from the swimming.

He leads me right to the bed as we enter his room. He's right—it is an enormous bed.

I let go of his hand and reach for his shoulders. He gives me a quick kiss on the lips before stepping behind me and kissing the back of my neck.

His hands massage my shoulders and down my back, pressing lightly against my spine with his thumbs. His lips place gentle kisses along each side of my neck and behind my ears as his hands sculpt over my back.

Ian places both of his hands over my abdomen with his fingers splayed and urges my back against his front. I drop my head back against his shoulder as his hands cup my breasts.

His fingers deftly unbutton my gold silk blouse to below my bra, exposing the emerald satin and lace. With the lightest touch, he traces his fingers over my breasts as if he were memorizing every inch.

My blouse falls open further as he tugs it from my pants and unfastens the remaining buttons. His warm hands skim over my flesh as his mouth leaves a trail of heat down the back of my neck and over my shoulders.

The fabric slips down my arms and drifts to the floor. Ian flattens one of his hands against my lower abdomen while the other unhooks my bra. He kisses a path down the middle of my back. A shiver of need races through me as his erection presses against me through his jeans.

He removes my bra. One of his hands plucks at my nipples while the other keeps my hips tight against his.

I reach back and clutch his head as his mouth returns to my neck. I angle my head to reach his lips.

His tongue dives into my mouth as his fingers unclasp and unzip my pants. I want his skin on mine. I grasp the collar of his T-shirt and tug. He lifts his head and yanks the shirt off, then tosses it to the side before returning his hands and lips to me.

Ian's heated skin rubs against mine. The thump of his heartbeat pulses against my shoulder as our tongues duel and his fingers slip inside my panties.

My breath catches as pleasure zings from my core.

I spin in his arms and attack the fastening on his jeans. Playtime is over. My need is too great.

He backs me toward the bed while giving me intoxicating kisses. He groans into my mouth as I free his erection from his jeans.

Ian yanks down the bedding, sending the decorative pillows flying. He opens the drawer on his nightstand and removes a condom while I shove off my pants and panties. He watches me while I recline on his bed and he shucks off his jeans and underwear.

"I've imagined you here. The reality is better than the fantasy."

I hold out my arms to him, and he covers me with his body, kissing me until we're both breathless.

He dons the condom while I watch and trail my fingertips up his thighs.

Our gazes lock when he enters me with ease. My heart thunders in my ears and the breath stutters from my lungs as we move together in a driving rhythm.

His head rests in the cradle of my neck, and I drag my lips along his cheekbone and clutch him to me.

Sensual bliss engulfs my body, and I soar toward the ultimate gratification. My breath stops and my eyes close as I reach the height of fulfillment.

Ian gasps and clutches me tighter as he surges inside me, reaching his own completion.

His harsh breaths puff against my ear. I hold his head, running my fingers through the thick hair at his nape.

My body sags into the mattress under his weight. I sketch one hand over his spine to the dip of his lower back.

"I'll have to retract my earlier assessment of your bed. It is indeed better than average. In fact, I might even go as far as to say it's spectacular."

He lifts his head. "For that you deserve a reward."

"Oh? You're up to reward me some more?"

"I will be after our bath...or during our bath."

He kisses me, then stands. I watch him walk into the bathroom. I stretch among the luxurious soft sheets as the sound of water filling the tub drifts from the bathroom. I grin.

This friends-with-benefits thing just might work out after all.

CHAPTER 22

"*I*t's not working!" Drew bellows as he slams his bedroom door repeatedly.

I focus on keeping my voice even and calm. "Your phone will work again once the battery charges. We just need to find your charger." I already checked the car, his backpack, and I even tore his bed apart looking for it.

"I don't know where it is!" He punches the doorjamb.

I managed to figure out his phone had died in the middle of his game when I heard him curse and then the phone flew down the hall to land at my feet as I ran from the bathroom. Hopefully, once I locate the charger it will turn on and not be permanently damaged from the fall.

I close my eyes and take a breath. I meant to buy another charger when the last one broke and he started using the only backup I had left, but it slipped my mind. I pinch the bridge of my nose. If I hadn't upgraded my phone this year, we would have compatible chargers and I could just use mine. *Where the hell could he have left it?*

"I'm going to throw it out the window!"

I clench his phone in my hand. "No, you're not. If you do, then it will be broken beyond repair. I need you to calm down so I can continue looking for your charger."

"No, give it to me! I don't care!"

He lunges toward me. I back up several steps. A dark blur rushes past me.

Ian stands between me and my brother. He shoves Drew back.

Drew stumbles against the frame of his door and raises his fist.

Ian takes a step forward.

I lurch between them and slap a hand against Ian's chest. "What the hell are you doing? Don't you ever lay hands on my brother! Get the hell out!"

Drew's bedroom door slams shut behind me.

Ian scowls at the door and back to me. "I'm not going anywhere until I know you're safe. Your brother is twice your size. He was charging you. I heard him yelling from the parking lot. Has he hurt you before?"

"I knew this wasn't going to work. You need to leave. What are you even doing here? This is none of your business."

"I brought a pizza. And it is my business. You're my business."

"No, I'm not. I mean it. Get out. I don't have time for this or you."

I swing around and gingerly open Drew's door. He's on the floor by his bed, rocking back and forth.

I kneel on the floor. "Drew, honey, everything is okay. I'm going to go look for your charger. I'll get your phone working and then you can play your game, but I need you to calm down so I can do that."

He continues to rock, staring at the wall across from him.

I stand and back out of the room. "I'll search in the living room. You stay here, okay?"

There's no response, but I didn't expect one.

I turn around. Ian is leaning against the wall with his arms folded over his chest. I glare at him and stalk past. I can't forcibly make him leave, and Drew is my priority. I don't want to agitate him more by fighting with Ian.

There's a pizza box on the floor by the front door. I ignore it and continue to the living room. I scan every surface, looking for the missing charger. Nothing. Where the hell did he leave it?

I toss the cushions off the couch and onto the floor. Ian walks into the room. I suppose I could call the police and have him removed, but that would lead to a lot of attention and scrutiny I don't want or need.

Dropping to all fours, I search under the couch. A royal blue cord winds like a snake by the wall.

Thank God! I lay flat on the ground and stretch my arm underneath and snag the end. Ian is watching me when I climb to my feet.

"Not one word," I mutter as I give him a wide berth and walk back to Drew's room. I pull his phone from my back pocket where I stuffed it when he tried to grab it from me.

"Drew, look! I found your cord." I plug it into his phone and then walk over and plug the other end into the outlet.

Drew stops rocking and looks at me and his phone. I glance down, waiting to see if it will turn on. I should have plugged it in out there and checked it before bringing it in here. If it doesn't come on, it could trigger another meltdown.

The symbol comes on the screen, and the phone dings. I sigh in relief.

"It needs to charge for a bit before you can play it."

"Can I play it while it charges?"

"Yes, but give it a few minutes first."

"Okay." He scoots over to lean against the wall next to the outlet.

"Drew, do you have something to say to me?"

He gives me a shy smile. "Thank you."

I stare at him, waiting for him to process what he needs to do.

"Sorry."

"We're going to have to talk about the consequences of your behavior later. What you did is not okay. You can't threaten people, and you can't damage property when you get upset."

"I know." He picks up his phone and cradles it in his hands.

I rub my forehead. "Okay."

I close my eyes and huff out a breath. Now I have to go deal with the other angry male—unless fortune is finally smiling down at me and he left like I told him to.

He didn't.

Ian stands at the intersection of the hallway, entryway, and living room with his arms still crossed over his chest. The pizza box is no longer on the floor.

Why did he pick this night to drop by unannounced?

I press my lips together and shake my head. It doesn't matter. It was bound to happen eventually.

"I told you to leave—twice, if I'm not mistaken. I'm tired, and I have nothing left to say to you. I don't want to upset Drew further by arguing with you."

"Then don't argue. Listen."

I fold my arms in front of my waist.

"I apologize for overreacting, but please try to look at it from my perspective. I heard yelling and what sounded like a fight. I thought you were in trouble...being attacked. I saw him charging at you with his hands raised. What was I supposed to do?"

"Not lay your hands on my brother. Do you think violence is going to teach him anything except more violence? I don't need you to save me. Do you really think shoving or hitting a special needs child when he has an episode is heroic?"

His head drops, and he stares at the floor.

Tears fill my eyes. "Look, I get it. You thought you were helping. This was my mistake. I knew better than to let you into our lives. It ends now. I want you to leave. Don't call me. Don't drop by. We'll go back to being acquaintances."

"That's it? One brief hiccup and you bail?"

"My brother is not a hiccup," I hiss at him.

"You know that's not what I meant." He runs his fingers through his hair and holds the back of his head. "You went into this expecting us to fail. You're jumping on this as an excuse to end it. I apologized for my reaction. I didn't think. I saw you being threatened, so I reacted."

"That's the problem, Ian. What's going to happen the next time? Or the one after that?" I throw my hands up as the tears overflow my eyes. "I cannot handle a relationship with you. I told you that from the start. My plate is full. Hell, it's overflowing and cracking right down the center."

I wave my hand between us. "Relationships are work. I told myself this wasn't one, but I was lying to myself. For the sake of my brother and my own sanity, I need you to leave. Please."

I can't look at him, so I stare at the floor as the tears streak down my face.

A moment passes before his feet walk by and the front door opens and closes.

If I had locked the door after running down to search the car for the cord, this wouldn't have happened. A sob escapes me. I brace a hand against the wall as my shoulders shake.

The wall is cool as I rest my cheek against it and muffle the sobs with my hand.

I shove off the wall and half jog to the living room. I snort back pain and scrub the tears from my face.

The pizza box sits on the counter in the kitchen. It's gluten-free. He remembered Drew is gluten-free.

I sink down onto the couch cushions strewn on the floor, curl into a ball, and cry.

CHAPTER 23

*K*elly's assistant points to a door in the back corner I've never noticed before. "She said for you to go on back."

"Thanks." The door is hidden behind a mirror. It opens to a narrow room. Kelly sits at a sewing machine with bright red material draped all over it.

I lift the bag of takeout I picked up on my way over. "I come bearing lunch. I need someone to vent to. Interested?"

"Always." She stands and waves me in. There's a table stacked with fabric and miscellaneous doodads. She clears off half the space and swings another chair over to the end. "Voilà."

"I got Chinese because it was quick and I have a craving for sesame chicken and egg rolls. I hope you like it. We can order something else if you don't."

"My favorite."

"Good." I set out the containers and plop down in the chair.

I chomp off a piece of egg roll and chew unenthusiastically.

"Spill it. Did something happen with Ian?"

I inspect the inside of the egg roll. "What makes you think it has something to do with him?"

She sighs and opens a container. "Rebecca, you two practically light fires when you look at each other."

I shrug and drop the egg roll down on my plate. My appetite is nonexistent. "We agreed to a friends-with-benefits arrangement."

"How's that going for you?"

I brush the crumbs off my fingers. "It was going fine, but I ended it last night."

She sets down her fork with a piece of chicken on it and rests both of her palms on the table. "Why?"

"Because it was never going to work. He walked in on Drew having a meltdown and got physical with him." I tell her all the sordid details, watching her reaction to each piece. Someone who doesn't have experience with a meltdown might not understand. I thought about talking to Kerry, but she's teaching at the school, and I couldn't wait until I had a babysitter and was able to schedule a get together. Franny is still in the middle of the Mediterranean on her honeymoon, hopefully having the time of her life.

Kelly finishes chewing the bite of chicken. "He thought he was protecting you—that your brother would hurt you."

I close my eyes and huff out a breath. "I know that."

"Has he hurt you?"

I pop my eyes open. "No."

She rolls a paper napkin between her fingers. "Are you ever afraid he will?"

I press my fingers between my eyes. "Of course I am. I realize there's the possibility. We go to a therapist with experience with autism. Drew goes alone and we have appointments together as well because he doesn't exactly share the incidents without a lot of prompting. He's getting better at handling his anger. The outbursts are shorter and he recovers quicker."

I take a drink of my soda. "None of that is the point though."

This was supposed to be a vent session about Ian, not an interrogation.

"I know you're upset about Ian, but you're my friend and I want to make sure you're safe. I can't claim to understand your brother's behavior or the right way to handle it. I imagine Ian doesn't have experience with these types of meltdowns either."

"You think I was wrong to be angry with him and tell him to leave?" I fold my arms over my waist and lean back in my chair.

"No, you were protecting your brother, who is basically your son. You're wired to ensure his safety and attack anyone and anything that tries to harm him, as a mother does." She picks up her fork. "I do think you should give Ian another chance though."

I stare at her. Did she not hear what I said?

I throw my hands up. "What would be the point? It can't lead anywhere. Even if we get past this meltdown, there will be more. Or there'll be a multitude of other things."

She frowns and takes a bite of her chicken, staring at me while she chews and swallows. "You sound pretty sure it's doomed."

I cross my legs and tap the bottom of my shoe against my heel. "I had a boyfriend when my parents died. We'd dated a couple of years. We lived together and were talking about getting engaged. You know the whole love fairy tale."

Kelly stares at me while scooping up another forkful of food. "I take it the relationship didn't end well?"

"He told me it was him or Drew. I mean not in those exact words. He went on about a special home for kids like Drew being the right thing to do—for Drew, of course. That he would be better off in a place like that than with a kid barely out of college and just starting her life."

"I hope you gave him a piece of your mind while you kicked his ass out the door."

"I lit all his clothes on fire."

Kelly widens her eyes. Her mouth opens and then turns into a grin. "Did you really?"

"Yup. Granted it was after the *discussion* had been going on for over an hour for the fourth or fifth time. I think he believed he could convince me he was right by talking me to death. He followed me from room to room and then told me I was being selfish. I grabbed the laundry basket of his clothes which I had washed and folded for him, snagged his lighter from the kitchen table, and walked right out the front door."

I roll my eyes and shake my head. "He kept talking the entire time. He didn't start screaming at me until his clothes were in the middle of a bonfire on the front lawn. Then he called me a crazy bitch and told me he didn't want to have anything to do with my mentally damaged family."

"That son of a bitch!"

"Actually, his mother was a very sweet woman."

Kelly shakes her head and snorts out a laugh.

"I threw the rest of his things out the front window—everything that I could jam through anyway."

"Good for you. What did he do?"

"He screamed he was going to get the police and have them arrest me. He ran down the road to—I assume—his buddy's house to make the call since his phone was still inside with me."

"Did he really call the police?"

I shrug. "I don't know. I grabbed my suitcase, stuffed a bunch of my things inside, and left. It was his house after all."

Kelly chuckles and drinks her water.

Jeff hadn't shown his true colors until then. He had been a kind, affectionate, considerate boyfriend. I thought I was going to marry him and raise a couple of kids together.

My baggage is too much for a man to handle.

"I get you've been burned, but you can't judge all men by one selfish asshole."

"That's just it though—he wasn't like that until my parents died."

"You just didn't see it until things got difficult and didn't go his way. Ian already knows you and Drew are a package deal. Don't write him off completely. He doesn't strike me as the type to turn and run when things get difficult."

"It was only a friends-with-benefits arrangement."

"Uh-huh."

I glare at her over my soda.

"If that's all it was, why are you so upset it ended?"

"Because the sex was amazing."

She chokes on her drink and laughs. "Good to know, but that's not all."

"How do you know?"

"I've seen you smile more, laugh more, the past few weeks. Not that you aren't a friendly person normally, but you seem lighter. Happier. I think it has a lot to do with Ian."

"Again, the sex was amazing."

"Yeah, yeah, brag to the single lady that hasn't gotten any in longer than she cares to think about. If sex was all it was, you wouldn't have let him near Drew."

Well shit! She might be on to something.

CHAPTER 24

"*I* know you're in there. I can hear you breathing on the other side of the door."

Can he really? I hold my breath and peek out the peephole at Ian standing on the landing outside my apartment.

He hasn't shaved in a day or two. His dark hair falls haphazardly around his ears and forehead instead of combed back and styled.

"I can also see the light shift underneath your door."

I sigh.

"You've ignored all my calls and texts. I didn't think you'd react well to me showing up at your shop or apartment when Drew was home, so I waited until Monday when I knew you'd be more likely to be home and alone."

He's right. I would've felt ambushed at the store, and I don't want to talk to him with Drew around.

I drop my head against the door. I'm not prepared for this. I thought we said all there was to say...or at least, what I wanted to say. Kelly made me rethink my perspective. The right thing to do is to hear what he has to say. It doesn't mean anything is going to change. I haven't changed my mind. A relationship still isn't a good idea.

Hell, maybe I'm overthinking this. He might just want to vent or tell me off. He's probably not interested in pursuing me anymore.

"Please, Rebecca?"

I heave a sigh and unlock the door. It's better to rip the bandage off, right?

His gaze scans me from head to toe as I open the door.

It's my day off and I wasn't planning for company. My lounging pajamas are comfortable, damn it.

"Thank you for opening the door."

"I'm not sure what there is left to say."

He stuffs his hands in the front pockets of his jeans. "I'd like you to hear me out."

"Okay." I fold my arms in front of me.

"I'm sorry. I never should have put my hands on him. I would still get in front of you to block any threat, but I've given this a lot of thought all week. It's pretty much all I've thought about."

He sighs and lifts his shoulders. "I did a bunch of online research and bought a few books to try and educate myself on Drew and what to expect, what the meltdowns are, how to handle them...stuff like that. I'd like to learn more. According to what I read it's called a spectrum for a reason. No two autistic individuals are alike. I know Drew has other diagnoses as well, and I'd like to learn on how to properly handle and help him specifically."

I rub my arms. That was proactive and thoughtful.

"Look, I know I screwed up, and I know I don't know the right way to help and not hinder in that situation...but I'd like to learn. I'd like the opportunity to apologize to Drew. It kills me I might have scared him or damaged the friendship I have with him."

There are tears in his eyes. My mouth opens and closes as he rubs a hand over his face. I've been there more times than I could possibly ever count.

I step over and wrap my arms around him. He squeezes the breath from me in a hug. His breath stutters as he inhales deeply. I feel his shudder in every pore of my body.

He sniffs and rests his head on top of mine.

Tears fill my eyes. I've been floundering since day one of becoming Drew's guardian. I didn't know what the hell I was doing. Still don't half the time.

I've screwed up and felt the guilt eviscerate me.

I snuggle against his chest as my tears dampen his shirt. He kisses the top of my head and gives me a squeeze. He rubs my back soothingly. We stand like that for several minutes.

I lift my head and wipe my cheeks.

Ian tucks my hair behind my ear and uses his thumbs to dash the remainder of my tears away. "I really am so sorry."

"I know." I reach up and cup his cheeks. They're damp from tears.

"I've shed an ocean full of tears over the years over Drew. Not just when I've felt helpless, but when I've felt guilt and shame because I've lost my temper with him. I'm still learning the right ways to support him and help him. I don't always know the best way to act or proceed."

"You're an incredible woman. He's lucky to have you."

"I hope so, but I'm the lucky one. He's taught me so much. He really is the best person I know. He has a heart of pure gold. He's my gentle giant. I know it doesn't seem that way when he has a meltdown, but it's because his brain can't handle the overload of stimuli. It's not his fault, and he does feel remorse after."

"When I saw him rocking back and forth on the floor, it broke my heart. I didn't understand any of it until I read about triggers and processing and the shutdowns."

"How could you? Unless you live it, it's hard to comprehend."

"Will you allow me to apologize to him?"

I nod. "I think it would be good for both of you. Drew really likes you."

"Even after last week?"

"Drew doesn't hold on to things like most people. He doesn't hold a grudge. Even though he has a memory that astounds me, he seems to forget all about the meltdowns shortly after they occur." I shrug. "I can't really explain it. Once the meltdown is over. He'll apologize. Even though it's often with prompting, he's getting better at initializing it. Once he does that, it's like a switch flips and he immediately moves on."

"Not a bad skill to have, actually. People tend to hold grudges way too long."

"I definitely can hold a grudge."

He laughs. "I know." He takes my hand. "Can you forgive me?"

"I've already forgiven you, Ian."

"But? I can tell there's a but."

"I told you I don't date. I don't do relationships. I thought we could keep it casual, but clearly, I was fooling myself. It just can't work."

"You said you don't date because you don't have the time. I'm not putting any pressure on you to take away from work or Drew. I can work around your schedule."

"That's understanding of you, but time isn't the only issue." I throw my hands up. "I like you, obviously. It was recently pointed out to me that if it was just sex, then I never would have let you be around Drew. It's true. I own that, but I've tried dating before and it's always a disaster. I was in a long-term relationship when my parents died. Long story short, he didn't want me to become guardian of Drew. I ended it. He wasn't the only one. Every single time I've tried dating a guy, he would eventually expect me to choose between him and my brother. Not once. Not twice. Every single time. So, I promised myself no more dating until Drew is old enough and mature enough to be a little more independent and not need me twenty-four seven."

Ian scowls and folds his arms over his chest. "Now I understand your comment about having horrible taste in men. You dated spineless assholes. I'd appreciate not being lumped into the same category as them."

I drop my face into my hands and groan.

He puts his hands on my waist. "We were always dating, whether you put the label on it. I'm willing to compromise to make this work. We can go as slow as you need. I won't pressure you. If I do, I'm sure you'll call me out on it and put me in my place in a heartbeat. I don't want to give up on us before we even have a chance."

I lower my hands and stare up at him. "You really are a charming devil, aren't you? Did you read books on how to talk to a woman too?"

"Naw, that comes naturally."

I plop my head in the middle of his chest and groan.

He massages my shoulders. "Say yes."

"There will have to be rules."

He laughs and his chest shakes beneath my forehead.

"Of course there will be. You can make me a list. Would you like that?"

I lift my head and glare up at him. "It will be a very long list."

CHAPTER 25

How could I have mistaken Ryan for Ian? Sure, there's a resemblance and they're obviously related, but Ian is clearly the more handsome of the two. There was low lighting in the pub that night and I'd been standing across the room. My brain expected to see Ian, so it must have filled in the details. I would never mistake Ryan for Ian now.

Ian and his brothers toss a football around with Drew. He's laughing and throwing his head back delightedly. I never knew he had such a throwing arm. Of course, I never thought to throw around a football with him either.

"Handsome bunch, aren't they?"

Rose sits in the red Adirondack chair next to me. We're situated around the fire pit in Ian's backyard. She's an attractive woman. I'm guessing she's in her mid to late fifties if she's married to Ian's dad, since Ian mentioned his parents were both in their early sixties. Although she could be significantly younger than he is. There's barely a line on her face, but I guess nowadays that's hardly a tell with all the cosmetic enhancements available. She doesn't strike me as the type to care about that though. There isn't a trace of makeup on her ivory skin, and her blonde hair is generously streaked with gray.

"They certainly are." I glance back at the men.

"My Steve has blessed DNA, but your brother is a handsome young man too. I bet the young ladies think so too."

Do they? Oh God, I don't want to even contemplate that complication. Will Drew start having romantic interests? How will that play out? One more parenting role I am woefully unprepared for.

I tilt my head to the side and study him. "He's a combination of both our parents."

Her husband sits in the chair next to her and smiles at both of us.

"How come you're not out there playing?"

He winks at his wife. "I will once they tire themselves out a little more. I need to even the playing field."

Susan plops down in the chair next to me. "Sound plan. I might join you. I prefer baseball, but football has its merits.

"I have no sports ability whatsoever. I was always the last one picked in PE class."

Rose pats my hand. "I'm with you, Rebecca."

I smile and glance over my shoulder at the house. "Are you sure Molly doesn't need any help?"

Ian's mother shooed me out of the kitchen when Drew and I arrived. I deposited the box of desserts I'd picked up at The Sweet Spot and wandered outside where she directed us. Ian greeted me with a kiss and introduced me to Ryan; Mike's girlfriend, Tammy; and Conner's girlfriend, Leslie.

Tammy had been pleasant enough, but she soon got a phone call and disappeared inside. Leslie still lounged in a bikini by the pool. She hadn't done more than wave from her lounge chair when we were introduced. The men decided to play football so I wandered over here to watch.

Susan waves her hand. "Molly doesn't like anyone else in the kitchen—whether it's hers or not." She chuckles. "As you can see, she even kicks Ian out of his own kitchen and he is a chef."

I never thought of him as a chef before, but I suppose he is. He's a marvelous cook. He's spoiled me with more than one delicious meal over the past few weeks.

I prop my sandal on top of the unlit fire pit. The summer sun bathes my skin in warmth. A hum sounds to my right. A hummingbird with a bright green chest hovers over a rose of Sharon bush covered in pink flowers at the corner of the black iron fence surrounding the pool.

"What perfect weather for the holiday. It rained the last Independence Day, didn't it?" Rose frowns and glances at Steve.

His dark eyebrows bunch together and he looks at Susan. "I think you're right. Last year we were at the farm, weren't we?"

Susan rests her head against the back of the chair, her face tilted toward the sun, and closes her eyes. "Nope, that was the year before. It poured, so we all grabbed what we could and headed for the barn."

"That's right. They postponed fireworks on the lake that year. Where were we last year?" Rose wrinkles her nose as she stares at Susan.

"Your house."

Steve lets out a bellow of laughter, and Rose drops her head into her hands.

Susan shakes her head and laughs. "Conner brought that girl— Betty, Brenda… Something with a B. She was so busy taking selfies of herself she fell in the pool fully clothed and demanded he take her home."

"Oh Lord, how could we have forgotten that?" Rose gasps and covers her mouth with her hand.

"We never saw that one again, did we?"

Rose twists her head and glances at the pool where Leslie remains. "I don't think so."

"Don't worry. She can't hear a thing. She's got those earphones or whatever they're called stuck in her ears." Susan glances at me. "Conner changes girlfriends frequently."

"At least he brings them around to meet us. I can't remember the last girl I met of Ryan's." Steve stares up at the blue sky. "Rebecca, you're the first girlfriend of Ian's I've met since he was in high school, I think."

"Really?" I'll have to ask Ian why that is. Why am I the first girl-friend he's introduced? Has he not dated exclusively?

All three of them nod.

"Mike has dated Tammy for years, but she works a lot so he's often at family gatherings alone." Susan jerks her chin toward the yard.

Tammy is coming down the path from the beach and Mike's house. When had she left?

"What does she do?"

"Surgeon."

"I imagine it's a demanding profession." I glance at Tammy, still on her phone, strolling across the yard.

"She's ambitious too. Wants to run the whole damn hospital one day, I think. She's jockeying for head of her department so she can add it to her résumé and land a position at a more prestigious hospital." Susan folds her arms over her abdomen and rests her bottle of beer on her stomach.

"Impressive."

"Depends on your priorities."

Sounds like Susan isn't a fan of Tammy. They do work at the same hospital. Maybe she's seen or heard things as a nurse that she doesn't agree with.

"What does?" Molly scoots around the occupied chairs to the free one next to her wife.

"Just filling Rebecca in on the girlfriend situation among the boys."

Molly winces and playfully slaps at Susan's hand. "Don't scare her away. Ian will never forgive us."

"What's scary about knowing what she's walking into? I'd rather know what's what than walk in uninformed."

"Hmm. Maybe you're right. Anything you want to know, Rebecca, feel free to ask."

I chuckle. "I'll keep that in mind, thanks."

Molly glances behind her at the men. "I do worry about Ryan though. Do you think he prefers boys to girls? Should I talk to him?"

Susan chokes on her beer. "You really think he'd have a problem telling *us* if he was more interested in men?"

"I suppose you're right."

"Don't fret, Molls. I caught Ryan with more than one girlie magazine when he was a teenager. He's not keeping some enormous secret from us."

Molly grimaces at Steve. "I really didn't need to have that image in my head."

"I saw Ryan with a blonde several weeks ago, and they were extremely friendly, if you know what I mean."

"I thought today was the first time you met Ryan."

I glance at Rose. "It was. I had gone into Flannigan's Pub and saw them. I mistook him for Ian at the time, which I know is ridiculous because they don't look much alike, but the lighting was dim and I was distracted."

"Not look anything alike?" Rose frowns and looks from me and then over to where they're still playing.

Molly grins. "Most people can't tell Ian and Ryan apart. Rose still has a tough time. They are identical twins after all."

I stare as Ryan throws to Drew, who catches the ball but drops it and stumbles after it. Ian jogs over and shows him how to tuck the ball into his chest.

They have the same dark hair, but Ian is more muscular, making him seem taller by at least an inch. Ryan's eyes are nowhere as bright, and they don't have the depth of color Ian's do.

Identical? How is that possible?

"I've been able to tell them apart since birth, but they have fooled other family members a time or two."

Steve raises his glass. "That would include me, and I'm their father. I used to think Molls was bluffing she could tell them apart so easily. It wasn't until they started talking it got easier for me."

"It took me a couple years too. If they deliberately try to fool me, however, I'm hopeless. They get me every time. They haven't tried in quite a while though." Susan snickers.

Molly reaches over and clasps Susan's hand. "That might have something to do with the way you retaliate when they do."

"True." Susan grins.

Steve lets out a guffaw and glances at me. "She filled their tooth-paste with blue food dye! Their teeth were bright blue for days."

"Didn't you let the air out of the tires of their cars too?"

Susan nods at Rose. "Sure did. The teeth were my favorite though."

Molly shakes her head. "She drove several hours round trip to get to Ryan's tires. You are tenacious, my love."

"Got you, didn't I?"

"Yes, you did."

I cringe. "Remind me never to make you mad."

"Telling you about all the ways she got her revenge against my innocent brothers and me?" Ian strides over and kisses me on the head as he leans on the arm of my chair.

"Innocent? You and your brothers have never been innocent." Steve claps his hands and rubs them together.

"We learned from the best, Dad." Ryan drops into one of the last empty chairs. There are eight circled around the stone firepit. Mike wanders over to where Tammy still talks on the phone on the other side of the pool, and Conner joins Leslie poolside.

I glance over to where Drew is sitting on the ground about twenty feet away.

"He found a caterpillar." Ian chuckles. "Said he had to go find a safe home for it."

"He loves creatures big and small."

Ian leans close and whispers in my ear, "Having a fun time?"

I nod. This dating thing hasn't been so bad. He cooks. He's great in bed. He doesn't push for more than I'm ready for. He and my brother get along wonderfully. Ian has even asked about going to a therapy session with us so he can learn more about how to support Drew.

Maybe my luck is changing for the better. Only time will tell.

CHAPTER 26

"*H*i, Becks."

My breath stutters and stops. It's like a brick to the chest. Rachelle stands inside the door of Blossoms, dressed in a pair of faded jeans and a black tank top. Her brown hair reaches her waist. It had been just below her shoulders the last time I saw her.

She's thinner—leaner. All the baby fat is gone. Twenty-six years old now, so that's not surprising. I blew out a candle on a cupcake in January like I do every year on her birthday.

Her hands are stuffed into the back pockets of her jeans. She hasn't moved from the door.

"Hello, Rachelle." Below the counter, I rub my damp palms on the front of my skirt.

She bites her lip and steps forward.

What is she doing here after all these years? Why now? Does she need money?

Visions of her snatching the check out of my hand and screaming "Just because we share the same blood, it doesn't make us a family" into my face burst through my mind.

I flinch and stare down at the countertop as tears fill my eyes. I haven't known if she was alive or dead for years. I imagined the worst on many occasions and grieved. Which was worse: imagining her dead or knowing she was alive and not caring enough to let us know?

"Where have you been?"

"Europe, mostly. Most recently California."

She stands in front of the counter now. I scan her familiar features. She looks just like Mom.

I look at the ceiling and wipe a tear from my cheek.

"I like your store. I never pictured you as a florist or a store owner. I thought you'd be running some Fortune 500 company or something."

She picks at the corner of a sign displaying what credit cards I accept taped to the front of the cash register.

"Plans changed."

"Yeah." She stuffs her hands back in her pockets.

"What are you doing here, Rachelle?"

"I wanted to see you and Drew."

"Why now after eight years?"

"I wanted to before, but the longer I stayed away, the harder it got to come home." She peeks at me then looks at the floor. "I did once. A few years back I went to New York, to the house. I didn't knock on the door or anything, but I waited in my car across the street. A family came out."

"I sold the house a couple years after they passed away. It was too much to maintain."

She nods. "It looked different. They painted it white and cut down that gigantic tree in the front yard."

Her gaze darts around the store. "I talked to Jane. She told me where you moved to."

She talked to our cousin, and Jane didn't tell me? Didn't warn me?

"When?"

"Last week."

Jane is going to get a phone call from me. How could she not tell me?

"Have you been in touch with her all these years?"

"No. I showed up unannounced at her house last week. She gave me an earful about taking off the way I did. Shook me a few times, then hugged me and cried all over me."

"That sounds like Jane." She has a big heart, and I wouldn't expect her to turn Rachelle away, but I would expect her to call and give me a heads-up and tell me my long-lost sister is not only still alive but is about to waltz back into our lives.

"How's Drew? Jane says he's taller than she is now."

I stare at her a moment. She'd know how tall he is if she hadn't disappeared for the last eight damn years. What right does she have to ask about him after abandoning us without a word or letting us know she was even alive?

"He is."

"Becks." She reaches a hand over the counter toward me.

I flinch away and fold my arms over my waist.

"I'm sorry." She drops her hand to the counter and looks down. "I was so damn angry—not specifically at you—but at everyone and everything. You were the convenient target which bore the most of my anger."

"We were all upset. We should have had each other to lean on."

"I was eighteen."

"I was only twenty-two."

"Yeah, but you were the golden child who had everything figured out and did everything right."

"You were the spoiled brat with no responsibilities and no concept of the consequences of your actions." Golden child? I worked my butt off in school and out of it.

I may have known what I wanted back then—or at least what I thought I wanted, but I worked for it.

"Yeah, and I was the neglected middle child, always getting in trouble. The college dropout."

"You weren't neglected. Don't tarnish their memories."

Her eyes fill and she looks away. "I'm not. I wouldn't. I don't blame them, not anymore. They had their hands full with Drew. I didn't understand at the time. I resented him, them, everyone."

I drop my hands to the counter. "You were a kid."

"I am sorry for leaving you to handle everything. I know it wasn't fair. I know I said some awful things. I didn't mean them, Becks. I wanted to hurt you. I wanted to hurt everyone."

"You were grieving."

"Making excuses for me like always?"

I close my eyes. Mom and Dad had had their hands full with Drew, but Rachelle hadn't made things easy on them. She would stay out with her friends, get in trouble at school, and push buttons just to see what would happen. I told them she would grow out of it, that she was just being a rebellious teenager.

She rubs her palms on the front of her jeans. "I'd like to see Drew, if it's okay with you. He probably doesn't even remember me. He was only eight when I left."

No!

She can't just pop into his life again after all these years. He's doing so well now. Losing our parents and then Rachelle had triggered so many meltdowns. It was a tumultuous time. What if letting her back into his life causes more upheaval?

If I say no, I'll be denying him a chance to reconnect with his sister. We have so little family left.

What's the right thing to do for Drew?

What would Mom and Dad want me to do?

I look down at Mom's ring as I spin it around on my finger. Each of our birthstones. Topaz for me. Garnet for Rachelle. Amethyst for Drew.

"He remembers," I whisper.

"He does?" I melt at the hope in her eyes.

"Still calls you Lola. He likes looking at the family photo albums. He'll point to a picture of you and ask when you're coming for a visit."

She presses her fist to her mouth as tears overflow her eyes.

I walk around the counter to the front door and flip the closed sign over and lock the door. The last thing I need is customers coming in. I walk back over and wrap my arms around my sister.

She breaks down and sobs in my arms as the tears flow freely from my eyes.

CHAPTER 27

"*Y*ou're letting me crash on your couch, so the least I can do is help out in your shop. I've worked in plenty of retail shops and restaurants over the years."

"You're family. I'll always have a place for you." She's told me a little about what she's been doing the past eight years, but only blanket statements like that one. Nothing long term for jobs or relationships, just a lot of moving around. It sounds like she would pick up and move somewhere else every time she got bored.

Rachelle rubs her palms together. "Thanks. Put me to work. How can I help?"

"If you don't mind, the displays could use a dusting. I have to go over the upcoming order and check some details for an appointment." The White Birch Inn has finally responded to my efforts to book an exclusive contract with them, and I want everything to be perfect.

"Sure, no problem."

I hand her the duster from underneath the counter and watch for a second while she gets to work. How long will she stay before she gets bored and moves on? And how will Drew handle it?

He'd been delighted with her arrival yesterday. There had been no hesitation or questions. He acted like she'd been gone a few days rather than years. Last night had been like old times. We'd had dinner as a family and talked while watching a show with Drew.

I walk into my small office in the back and grab my binder with the order information and go back out front in case any customers come in.

Drew had Rachelle put him on the bus for summer school this morning and asked if she would be there when he got home. That was the only sign he might wonder how permanent her visit is.

Should I ask her for more concrete details about her past or her plans for the future? Will that prompt her to disappear again if I push?

I bring up the website I use for ordering on my tablet.

For now, I need to concentrate on work and let things progress as they will with Rachelle. Drew's happy, and that's all I'm concerned with.

The bell rings on the shop door. A middle-aged woman I remember helping last week walks in and pauses as she scans the interior of the shop. Her gaze touches on Rachelle, who steps forward with a smile, before zeroing on me with a grimace. She stalks toward the counter.

I take a deep breath and paste a smile on my face. Something tells me this will not be pleasant.

"You sold me damaged goods!" She slaps her palms on the counter in front of me and jerks her chin in the air. The loose bun her brown hair is tucked into wobbles on the top of her head.

What is her name? Something common. She ordered a bouquet, so I don't know how she could claim it was damaged.

"I'm sorry you are unhappy with your flower purchase from last week. Can you tell me what's wrong with it?"

Perhaps I shouldn't have stressed she bought them last week, but she wouldn't be the first customer to expect the flowers to stay fresh forever. Although, she bought lilies, roses, and carnations, if I remember correctly, and they should last the week. Not much longer though.

Taylor! That's her name.

"They stink! My entire living room stank so bad I had to throw out the bouquet. Whatever you sprayed them with ruined them. I demand a refund." She slaps the counter again.

"Mrs. Taylor, I assure you I didn't spray them with anything. The lilies have a strong perfume once they open. Perhaps it was not to your liking?"

Some people find the scent too strong. Personally, I think it's heavenly.

She rears her head back as if I've offended her. Did I get the name wrong after all?

"You can't possibly expect me to believe that awful smell is natural. They smelled like death."

Okay, scents can be strong triggers for some people. Perhaps they brought back a memory of someone's funeral. Lilies are a common flower in funeral arrangements.

"Mrs. Taylor, I'll be happy to put together a fresh bouquet for you with no lilies. If you prefer a refund, I'll be happy to oblige."

A tiny white lie. I won't exactly be happy about it, but I don't want her to leave unhappy and broadcast her displeasure to everyone about me selling stinky flowers.

She purses her lips and then frowns. "Well, they were pretty, and I hate that I had to throw them out."

"I promise to create an arrangement without any powerful scents."

"Very well, but I'm telling you that smell was not natural."

I walk over to the cut flowers. Customers don't like being told they're wrong. It's best to smile and move them along—even if I have to bite my tongue and resist the urge to prove my point by thrusting a blooming lily under her nose.

The bell rings, and Ian walks in.

Rachelle sashays across the store with a flirty grin. "Hi there, handsome. What can I get for you?" She plants a hand on her hip and twirls the duster in her other hand. Her shoulders are thrown back, putting her cleavage on display.

Ian barely nods at her before his gaze lands on me and he grins.

A burst of delight spirals through me.

Not only at his obvious pleasure in seeing me, but his lack of interest in Rachelle or her considerable assets. I've always been a trifle envious of her endowment. I'm not completely lacking in that area, but her chest size is of centerfold proportions.

I hold up a finger to signal Ian I'll be with him in a moment and turn back to selecting flowers for Mrs. Taylor. All scent-free and long-lasting choices.

When I glance over as I walk back to the counter, Ian is frowning down at Rachelle and shaking her hand.

What's wrong? What is she saying to upset him?

I wrap up the bouquet and smile at Mrs. Taylor while my gaze darts between Ian and Rachelle.

"There you are, Mrs. Taylor."

She gives me a tight smile and sniffs the arrangement. Her smile loosens and she gives me a single nod. A tough lady to please.

"Have a lovely day. Enjoy the flowers."

She walks away without a word, the bouquet clenched in her fist.

I scoot around the counter and over to Ian and Rachelle as Mrs. Taylor leaves the shop.

Ian looks at me but doesn't smile. He doesn't greet me with a kiss.

I frown. I'd gotten use to those welcoming kisses. What's going on?

"Your sister introduced herself."

He can't possibly be upset I didn't rush over to do that. I was with a customer.

"Rachelle arrived yesterday. It was quite a surprise for Drew and me." I smile at her. "Rach, will you give us a minute?"

She beams at me. "Of course."

I glance after her as she scurries into the back. Why did that make her so happy?

Ah. I called her Rach instead of Rachelle. Could calling her by her nickname put the smile on her face? I'd never called her Rachelle growing up. It was always Rach, and I was Becks to her.

I haven't been able to stand anyone else calling me that for years. Could it be the same for her?

"You never told me you had a sister."

Is that what's bothering him?

"I haven't seen or heard from her in eight years. She took off after our parents died. It was not an amicable parting. I didn't know if she was alive."

"Eight years?"

The shock on his face is easy to discern. It's probably incomprehensible to him to not speak to one of his siblings for more than a week, let alone eight years.

"It's not a pleasant story. She was eighteen and angry. We were all fumbling in our grief."

"Where has she been?"

"She said Europe."

"She disappeared to Europe at eighteen?"

"That's what she told me yesterday."

"Did you look for her?"

My back stiffens. What did he think? I sent her off with a wave and a *see you later*?

"No, I threw a party. Of course, I looked for her. The police basically said there wasn't much they could do since she was eighteen and had left of her own free will. I badgered her friends, searched any hangouts I knew about. I even put up damn posters."

I shake my head and plant my hands on my hips. "I was twenty-two; my parents had just died. I had to explain to my eight-year-old special needs brother his mom and dad were never coming home. I had to handle their estate and rearrange my entire existence. So I guess I didn't do as much as I could have to hunt my sister down after she took her share of the life insurance money and told me sharing the same blood didn't make us a family."

He pulls me into his arms. "I'm sorry. I'm not judging you."

"Sure as hell feels like it," I mutter against his chest.

My arms are tight by my sides. I don't need to be judged by my boyfriend. I've had plenty of that in the past from previous

163

boyfriends. And those had claimed to love me. I left them to stew in their doses of self-righteous judgment and moved on with my life. No one has lived my life, and no one has a right to pass judgment on me.

"It surprised me to learn you have a sibling you haven't told me about...again. I overreacted. I'm sorry."

"Fine."

"That doesn't sound like a real fine. That sounds like a 'stop talking before I murder you' fine."

I snort. "It might be a little of both. I don't like to feel judged."

His chin rests on the crown of my head. "I promise you I wasn't judging you. I was stunned and wondering if there are any other siblings hiding somewhere or other secrets you don't trust me enough to share."

Sighing, I wiggle my arms free from his embrace and hug him back. "I'm used to handling everything on my own. I'm not prone to sharing every little detail about my life."

"I don't expect you to, but I would like to know the big items like missing siblings."

"I have no other siblings, or any family members...except for my cousin Jane I've mentioned before."

"Okay." He tilts my chin up by cupping my jaw. "Forgive me?"

I give him a mock scowl. "Perhaps."

Ian kisses me thoroughly and lifts his head. "How about now?"

I tilt my head and pretend to ponder the question. "Feeling slightly more inclined toward forgiveness."

He chuckles and kisses me again.

My mind fogs, and I grip his back in my hands as his mouth devours mine.

"Oops!"

The exclamation permeates my brain as Ian's lips linger on mine.

I pull back as I hear the storage room door shut.

Ian glances over my shoulder. "She's gone again. I don't suppose you want to come home with me and let me further convince you of my ardent apology?"

"Can't." I wave an arm around me. "Store."

"Right." He sighs. "I suppose your schedule got a little fuller. Why don't you give me a call when you figure out a time for us to spend time together? I'll take whatever I can get."

"I'm not sure how long she's staying. I want to spend time with her while she's here."

"I understand. How's Drew taking her reappearance?"

"Excited. He treats her like she's always been here."

"Good." He kisses me. "Call me."

"I will."

I move back behind the counter. Rachelle walks out of the storage area when the bell rings, signaling Ian's departure.

"Wow, Becks! I'm surprised the two of you didn't set off the sprinklers. He is hot. How long have you been an item?"

"Not long."

"I can stay with Drew so you can have some alone time with your man."

"I'll keep that in mind." It would be nice. Drew would probably love it. But we aren't quite there yet. One day back isn't enough for me to feel comfortable leaving her responsible for Drew for any length of time.

"I know it's going to take time for you to trust me. I left you to handle everything on your own. I'm here to help. Better late than never, right?"

Guess my poker face isn't as strong as I'd like.

"How long are you staying, Rach? Don't get me wrong, I'm glad you're here, but for Drew's sake I'd like to know if you're going to disappear abruptly." My sake, too, I suppose.

She stuffs her hands in the back pockets of her jeans. "I'll stay for as long as you'll let me. I have to get a job and a place to stay, but I want to stick around, if it's okay with you."

"Of course it's okay. The couch is yours, and I can hire you part time if you want."

Not sure how I'll swing the extra expenses, but if it helps her stay, I'll manage.

She smiles. "I appreciate the offer, but I'll need something full time, and crashing on your couch is great for a few nights, but I need my own place for the long term. Besides, you'll get sick of me if we live and work together."

"We have eight years to catch up on. I won't get sick of you."

She shrugs. "I'm used to living on my own."

"Okay." She plans to stay. That's a step in the right direction. We'll deal with everything else as it appears.

CHAPTER 28

"Wait." I hold my hand up. "Before we get sidetracked, I want to hear about Franny's honeymoon. I missed this month's book club because I didn't have a sitter, so I missed out on the details."

"Okay, but then I want to hear about this long-lost sister of yours." Franny points her fork at me. "Deal?"

Lucinda and Olivia both nod at me, wide-eyed. We finally coordinated our schedules and planned a girls' night together. I've only seen the three of them in passing since the wedding. There's never been time for much of a catch-up session.

Rachelle has settled into her new job as a waitress at Joe's Pizzeria and moved into one of the apartments above the restaurant. She's been here a couple weeks and seems to be settling in. When she offered again to watch Drew, I took her up on it. Ian was shorthanded at the pub and couldn't take it off, so I called the girls instead. If I happen to have my phone resting on the table where I won't miss a call or text from Rachelle or Drew, it doesn't mean I don't trust her with him. I simply need to be available in case something happens.

I tap my fingers on the screen, then look at the three of them spaced around the round table tucked into the corner of Joe's. "Yes, now spill."

Maybe I shouldn't have suggested we meet two floors down from Rachelle and Drew, but when Drew insisted he wanted to see her new apartment, how could I say no? It also allowed me to hear from Joe how great Rachelle was performing at her job.

The green plastic coating the booth creaks as I shift. There's a tear in the seat tickling the skin behind my knee every time I move. I tug my black shorts down to cover my skin, but they spring back in to place as soon as I let go of the material.

"Everything was perfect. The weather, the yacht, Mitch, the countries we visited. Did I say Mitch?"

Olivia and Lucinda laugh. I uncross my legs and scoot forward to prop my elbows on the table and concentrate on Franny's story rather than what might be happening upstairs.

"We visited several of the countries bordering the Mediterranean Sea. My favorites were Venice and this little medieval town perched on a hill in France. I loved walking the tiny cobblestone streets and discovering small shops tucked away."

She'd brought us all back little gifts. She'd delivered mine—a gorgeous silk scarf—to me at Blossoms after I missed the book club meeting,

"We took a romantic gondola ride in Venice. Mitch insisted I have the full experience. While there, he bought an exquisite glass sculpture of this sea nymph coming out of the water. He said it reminded him of me when I fell out of my kayak." She laughs. "You know it's true love then. I saw what I looked like after that dunking, and it wasn't a sea nymph."

"Aw, that's sweet." I take a bite of my pizza.

"We didn't do too many touristy things other than the gondola ride in Venice. We spent a few days anchoring off the coast of Greece. They have some beautiful beaches there, and I loved the white buildings, which are surprisingly cool despite the heat. It was relaxing and the best honeymoon I could dream of. I didn't even panic too much about the bakery because I knew Olivia could handle everything."

Olivia puts her hand on her chest. "I had enough moments of panic for the both of us and a brand-new appreciation of how hard you work to get all the product out. I know the customers are as thankful you're back as I am because you are the true artist. I can't accomplish the masterpieces you can even with your recipes."

"I'll second that. Olivia did an amazing job, but trying to manage it all ran her ragged. And I won't complain if I never have to get up before dawn again to mix ingredients." Lucinda raises her wine glass. "Here's to Olivia and Franny. I have crossed off working in a bakery with you from my list of potential jobs with a permanent marker. I don't mind filling in with the customers in front, but baking is not my calling."

"I didn't realize that was on your list, Luce." Franny clinks her water glass to her sister's wine glass.

"There've been a lot of jobs on my list. I crossed most of them off."

"You're great with the customers. I still think 'wedding planner' should be at the top of your list." Olivia winks at Lucinda. "You can officially start with mine."

"Actually, I was going to talk to you about that. I've been checking into what I'll need to do if I pursue a career as a wedding planner. I'll need to build relationships with local vendors if I'm serious about it."

"You've got two right here covered."

Lucinda smiles at me. "I know. It kind of seems like fate might be pointing me in that direction." She huffs out a breath. "So, Olivia, if you're sure you want to take a chance on a complete novice for one of the most important days of your life… I'm your gal."

Olivia bounces in her seat. "Yes!"

We all laugh as Olivia claps her hands.

"You heard the part about 'complete novice,' right?"

I touch her hand resting on the cushion next to me. "You're not. You did a wonderful job planning Franny's wedding."

Franny and Olivia both nod across the table.

"You're forgetting there was an official wedding planner for Franny's wedding. I simply helped."

"That's not exactly true, Luce. Sure, Mother hired the wedding planner, but you handled most of it. I don't even know why we kept the woman on until the end."

"She did a lot. You didn't see it because you went through me, and I went to her."

"Still, it was you who kept the wedding what Mitch and I wanted and not the monumental affair Mother wanted."

"I witnessed your planning firsthand at Blossoms. I dealt with you, not the wedding planner. You were not only thorough, but professional and creative. I think you'll make a terrific wedding planner *if* that's what you want to do."

"Thanks, Rebecca."

"I hope I'm not pressuring you into it, Lucinda. I'd love for you to plan my wedding, but if it's not something you want to do, I understand."

"Don't be silly, I'm just nervous and don't want to disappoint you. I wanted to make sure you know what you're getting into. I've already filled a notebook with ideas for your wedding."

Olivia grins. "Really? Did you bring it? I want to see."

"No, but you can drop by tomorrow after work."

"I'll be running up the stairs at five o'clock on the dot."

Franny taps a finger on her chin. "Maybe if it's not too busy tomorrow, Lucinda can stop by after the lunch rush and show us there so I can see too."

"Well, now, I feel left out." I smack the edge of the table.

Lucinda chuckles. "Don't worry. You and I will have plenty of time to go over everything when we work together on the flowers."

I wrinkle my nose. "Maybe I can sneak away from the store for a few minutes tomorrow. Let me know when you get together. Cat is off from college for the summer, so she's been taking more hours."

"I can't wait." Olivia picks up another slice of pizza from the center of the table.

"Your turn, Rebecca. What's up with your sister?" Franny leans back in her chair and folds her arms.

"I didn't know you had a sister." Olivia takes a bite of her pizza while Lucinda and Franny nod in my direction.

"I know, I know. Ian has already given me hell for being the woman with the secret siblings."

Franny chuckles. "Another subject we need to hear all the details on—you and Ian."

I tell them about Rachelle taking off after our parents' deaths and showing up eight years later. I leave out the gory details about the fights before she left and the wondering whether she was alive or dead for years.

"Holy shit!" Olivia cringes. "Don't tell my boys. They'll make me put money in the swear jar. I'm going to go broke."

"Girls' night is swear jar-free. It's like book club—what happens here is sacrosanct. We tell no one." Lucinda waggles her finger in the air.

"I was going to try a swear jar once, but then I realized I'd be the only one putting any money into it and I didn't need one more thing sucking the money out of my wallet."

Olivia points her folded pizza in my direction. "I wish I'd thought of that. My boys take way too much delight in catching me swearing. I think I'm alone and then one of them will pop out and say 'swear jar' in a singsong voice."

She puts her pizza down on her plate and wipes her mouth and fingers on her napkin. "I've got some news. Ollie is finally making the move and relocating to Granite Cove."

"Ooh, is that handsome brother of yours still single?" Lucinda bats her eyelashes at Olivia.

"Yes, but...don't take this personally, but I don't think Ollie is a right fit for you. Honestly, I wouldn't set my brother up with any of my friends. I love him to death, but he's not the relationship type."

"Who says I want a relationship?"

Olivia shrugs. "In that case, maybe he is your guy."

"Speaking of guys..." Franny looks at me.

"We're dating—getting to know each other."

"Haven't you known each other for well over a year?"

I frown at Lucinda. "Yes, but there's a difference between knowing someone casually and dating them."

"Casually? I thought you had sex with him," she says.

"A one-night stand does not translate to sharing all the intimate details of your life with them. At least not in my book. Maybe your experience is different."

"Actually, I've never had a one-night stand." She frowns and drums her fingernails on the table. "I should rectify that, shouldn't I?"

Franny chokes on her water.

"Uh…" Olivia glances at me.

"What? I'm not responsible for her deciding to have a one-night stand."

"It worked out for you."

"That wasn't my intention when it happened. I never thought I'd see Ian again. I certainly didn't think he'd be living in the same town. I'm not against them, but it depends on what you're looking for."

"What were you looking for?"

"A few hours of pleasure and to forget all my responsibilities and remind myself I was still a young, desirable woman."

"Sounds good to me." She looks over at Olivia. "What do you think? You think Oliver would be interested?"

"I think that goes without saying. You're gorgeous, but I really don't want to think of my brother having a sex with anyone—least of all one of my closest friends."

Lucinda wrinkles her nose. "That could get sticky."

"Gross!" Olivia covers her eyes with her hand while Franny and I burst out laughing.

"What?" Lucinda's gaze darts around the table at all of us. "Oh, that, too, but I meant complicated."

"Let's move past anyone having sex with my brother. Rebecca, you were telling us about you and Ian. Please continue."

"What do you want to know?"

"Do you love him?"

I blink at Franny. Love?

"Who said anything about love? We just started dating a few weeks ago." I rub the back of my neck, then straighten the napkin in my lap. Probably more like a couple of months, considering it's August.

"So neither of you have said the words to each other?"
"No."

CHAPTER 29

*D*immed lighting and a single red rose with baby's breath and greenery in a thin vase in the center of the table set a romantic mood. Though I would've selected a more original flower choice for the tables, the crisp white tablecloth and generous wine glasses are pleasant touches.

Ian sets his menu aside and takes my hand resting by my glass. "You've barely said a word since I picked you up. What's bothering you?"

Hmm, let's see. Franny mentioned the L-word last week, and now it keeps popping into my mind at odd intervals. I can't stop questioning whether that's the direction our casual relationship is heading or if I even want it to.

"Nothing. I just have a lot on my mind."

"Drew okay?"

"Yes, he's great, actually. His summer camp finished last week. He loved it and is already asking about going back next year. It's the first time in a long time he's called other kids his friends. I nearly burst out crying when he asked to invite a friend over. I've left a message with their parents about coordinating something for them to get together."

"Would that be Angelo?"

"Yes, did Drew tell you?"

"Not about the invite, but he mentioned him a few times while we were playing cars Friday night. Angelo likes cars too. They've traded a few over the summer."

"I wish he'd give a few away. He literally has giant bins full of them."

"Yeah, but I bet he knows exactly what he has."

"He does. His memory is astonishing." I rub my thumb over his hand. "I know I already thanked you, but you were a lifesaver hanging out with Drew on Friday so I could get the wedding order completed on time."

If he hadn't come through for me, it would've been a sleepless night. The flowers had been delivered late, so my arrangements had fallen behind. No one else had been available to watch Drew.

"Stop thanking me. I told you I'd be happy to help any time I can. I like hanging out with your brother. Not as much as I enjoy spending time with you, however. Remind me to get something special for your sister to thank her for allowing this rare night to ourselves."

"I gave her a large box of treats from The Sweet Spot. It's the only thing she would accept. It's the first time she'll have Drew overnight. She's been offering for a while, but I guess I've been paranoid."

"Understandable, since it's been just you and Drew for a long time. She hasn't been in his life. Does she know his routine and what to do if he has a meltdown?"

"Yes, we've been over everything, and I've left detailed lists. She remembers what he was like when he was little. He was inconsolable then. His meltdowns are actually much better now that he's older. It's only because he's so tall—man-sized—that they're intimidating. Rach has promised to call if something happens."

"Good."

I smile. He understands. I'm sure we'll both be disappointed if it happens, but at least I won't have to worry he'll be upset if it does.

"So, it's not Drew that's on your mind. Is it Rachelle?"

"Nope, all is good there too. She likes her job and her apartment. Joe raved about her when I had dinner there with the girls last week."

"You had dinner there?" He smirks. "That choice wouldn't have anything to do with Rachelle watching Drew at her apartment, would it?"

I stare at the tops of the ivory drapes flanking the window next to us and scrunch my nose. "If I say no, will you believe me?"

"It would be a hard sell."

"I felt guilty about it all night, but at the same time I felt better knowing I was right downstairs if anything happened."

"I'm surprised you've agreed to stay the night at my place clear across town."

"If I sneak out in the middle of the night, you'll know why."

"Wouldn't be the first time."

I wince. "Very funny."

The waiter takes our orders. I order the gnocchi, and Ian asks for the chicken marsala.

"You haven't told me what's occupying your thoughts."

"Probably just anxious over Drew and Rachelle's first sleepover. And we've got the summer festival next weekend. I've been juggling all the last-minute details and problems that keep popping up." I shake my head. "Never mind all that. Tell me what you've been up to? I've barely talked to you all week."

"What can I do to help with the festival? You don't need to do everything yourself. You're supposed to delegate."

"I am, and it's not that bad. Everyone is fairly organized this year, but someone is always asking about moving the location of their booth or the town hall has questions about permits." I wave my hand. "It's fine."

"How about I take over anything to do with the town hall? Would that help?"

"Yes, it would. Are you sure?"

"One hundred percent."

"Thank you. Seriously, let's talk about something else."

"Conner broke up with Leslie, and he crashed at my place for a few days because she kept showing up at his house and harassing him."

I set my glass down before taking a drink. "You're joking."

"Nope. He's blocked her phone number and on social media. She smashed his TV because she said he was paying more attention to it than her. He ended it, but she won't accept the breakup. I told him to file a restraining order, but I doubt he will. He's hoping she'll eventually give up."

"Wow. I don't know what to say to any of that."

"He likes them a bit crazy. He had one girlfriend who went through his photos and threw out any that had another woman in them. It didn't matter if he happened to be related to some of them. The box was in his closet too. It's not like he had them on display."

"Insecure."

"I guess. Another one tracked his whereabouts on his phone and hacked into his social media accounts and email."

"He might have a type, or he might choose women he knows will never last."

"Maybe."

"What about you?"

"What about me? Are you asking my type? That's easy. Sexy brunette with Guinness brown eyes, a killer wit, a marshmallow heart, and an astonishingly logical mind."

I roll my eyes. "Did you seriously just compare my eyes to a beer?"

He shrugs. "I own a bar, and it fits."

"I meant, we never talk about your past relationships. You know the basics of mine." Is there a reason he's never mentioned them? Is he pining over someone?

"That you've dated assholes before me?"

"Ha-ha." Unfortunately true.

"What do you want to know?"

I shrug. "I don't know. Anyone serious?"

"No."

"High school sweetheart?"

"I dated a few, but nothing serious. I cared more about sports then and in college."

"After college? You're, what, thirty?" *Please don't let him be younger than me. I don't want to be the older woman.* How has this not come up before now?

"Thirty-four. And I've dated some. The longest lasted about six months."

"Why did it end?"

"She wanted to move in together and get married. I didn't."

"No compromise?" A woman fell in love with him and wanted more so he ended the relationship entirely?

"She gave the ultimatum. I just gave her an answer she wasn't expecting. That was several years ago. I had just bought the pub, and my focus was on building my business. Marriage wasn't something I was ready to contemplate."

The waiter delivers the food. Each plate is easily enough to feed two or three people. The red sauce is fragrant and thick, with steam rising from the plate. My stomach rumbles.

"Anything else you'd like to know? Ask away. I have no secrets."

He holds his fork in one hand and a knife in the other as he watches me.

"Everyone has secrets."

He cuts into his chicken while I stir my gnocchi to help it cool.

"Fine, let me rephrase. I don't want to have any secrets from you, so if there's anything you want to know, ask."

"Thank you." I rest my hand on the table next to my plate. "If you want to ask me something, I'll do my best to answer too."

"Good to know. Ever live with a guy?"

"Yes."

"The one you were dating when your parents passed away?"

I nod and take a bite of my gnocchi. Yummy. Perfect little pillows of potato and flour in a rich sauce. Comfort food.

"How long did you live together?"

"Less than a year. I moved in with him after I graduated from college."

"How did your parents feel about that?"

After taking another bite, I lean back in my chair and frown. Did we ever have an actual conversation about it?

"I'm not sure. They never said anything either way. It really wasn't their way to meddle too much. I think Dad was surprised, and he probably wasn't thrilled his daughter was moving in with a guy, but he said nothing. He would've talked to Mom about it, and she would've smoothed his ruffled feathers, or if she'd agreed with him, then she would've talked to me. That's the way they worked. Mom was the one who dealt with the emotional stuff."

"You may or not have noticed, but both my parents and their spouses are all meddlers."

"You're a tight family. It's nice watching you together. My family was close, but not like yours. You talk to your family members daily, don't you?"

"Parents, yes. Brothers not every day. Not all of them anyway. We might shoot each other a text to check in if we're busy." He shrugs and laughs. "Okay, yes, if you include texting, I talk to all of them every day."

"See, I would talk to my parents a few times a week and see them at least once. I would come over for dinner or babysit Drew."

"What about Rachelle?"

"She was there occasionally, but she was the stereotypical moody teenager hiding in her room or out with her friends. The year she went away to college I barely saw her. She didn't come home much. I think she deliberately chose a college farther away so we wouldn't visit. Then she dropped out and moved home. My parents died a few months later."

"Why did she drop out?"

"Her grades were terrible. I'm not sure if it was too much partying and not enough studying, but I know she failed a couple classes. My parents threatened to stop paying tuition and make her go to a closer college where they could keep an eye on her. Instead, she dropped out of college altogether and said it wasn't for her."

"It's not for everyone."

"No, it's not. I'm not sure if she's figured out what she wants to do yet. Makes me a little nervous how long she'll stay, but even if she leaves, I think she'll stay in touch this time."

"What do you think is different?"

"Maturity, but also she's not the angry rebellious teenager she was."

"She seems to genuinely enjoy being in Granite Cove with you and Drew. I can see how much she loves the two of you and wants to make amends."

"She has nothing to make amends for. The past is the past. She was a teenager and grieving."

"There's that marshmallow heart."

I stir my gnocchi and sauce. Does he really believe I'm soft? Not one of my past relationships ever described me as such. The opposite, in fact. "Driven," "cold," and "distant" were commonly used—"bitch" being the common refrain at the ends of the relationships.

"You know, most people think I'm a bitch. You're the only one deluded enough to think I have a soft heart."

"No one who truly knows you thinks that. If you're referring to general perceptions, then those fools are just afraid of strong women."

I grin. "Damn, Ian. You are good for my ego."

"Finish eating so we can go home and I can show you what else I'm good for."

CHAPTER 30

*O*h *my God, I'm in love with Ian.*
I stare down at him. His eyes are closed and his head rests on the back of the couch. My gaze follows the exposed tan skin down his throat and to the parts of his chest his open shirt reveals. His chest still rises and falls rapidly, and there's a shine of sweat over his skin.

We never made it past the living room.

I still straddle his thighs, wearing nothing but my open blouse and bra. His pants are bunched at his ankles. His shoes are still on.

We made love. It can't be described as simply sex. Nothing that pleasurable, nothing that spiritual, could be described as "just sex."

Tears prick at my eyes. I don't want this feeling to end, yet it terrifies me at the same time.

How has he become such an integral part of my world? He brings me joy and comfort. He demands nothing from me except honesty.

I was so afraid a relationship would bury me in more responsibility, but instead it's freed me.

Ian helps, not hinders.

He eases my worries and bolsters my confidence.

I blink rapidly to clear away the dampness as his eyes open and his gaze ensnares mine.

"Hi, beautiful." His hands skim up my waist underneath my blouse.

"Hi, yourself."

"Ready to try and make it upstairs? It's entirely up to you because I'm more than comfortable right where I am." His fingers trace over my breasts.

"I think the bed might be a better choice this time."

"You sure?" He kisses the spot between my breasts

"Pretty sure."

He places a series of kisses underneath my breasts. "I suppose you're right. It will probably get chilly if we stay down here…eventually."

"Mm-hmm, and your bed is more comfortable."

He peeks down toward the floor. "I'd carry you, but with my pants around my ankles, I don't think we'd get very far."

I chuckle and swing a leg over to sit beside him instead of on his lap as visions of the bodily damage that could ensue if he were to attempt it flicker through my mind.

He kicks off his shoes and his pants after a swift tug and then stands and reaches for me.

"Huh-uh." I jump up and skirt around the coffee table. "I don't want either of us breaking any bones. How will we possibly explain?"

"Unbridled passion?" He lunges for me.

I jump away and dart for the stairs.

He catches me on the bottom step and swings me up into his arms.

I giggle—an honest-to-God giggle—as he carries me up the stairs and into the bedroom.

He tosses me onto the bed.

I yelp.

He removes his shirt and climbs on after me, then tugs at my blouse. "Why is this still on?"

I take it and my bra off and toss them to the end of the bed. "Are you sure at your advanced age you can perform a second time so soon?"

He narrows his gaze. "Is that a challenge, baby?"

I sit up and push on his shoulders. "Maybe you should lie back and let me do all the work this time."

He reclines on the pillow and folds his arms behind his head. "I will not argue with that."

I kiss my way across his chest and down the dark trail of hair in the center of his abdomen.

One hand cups my cheek, and I look up into his hot gaze.

His thumb brushes across my bottom lip. I suck on the tip, and he inhales sharply.

I smile and lower my head.

He loses all control within moments and lies panting on the bed.

I crawl up and lay my head on his chest. He enfolds me in his arms. His heartbeat thunders against my cheek.

I love you. The words form at my lips, but I seal my mouth closed.

What if he doesn't feel the same?

I don't want to be the first to say it.

I've said them to one other man, but I don't think I really meant them or knew what love was or could be. He was the first to say it. The words came too easily. I don't think he meant them, or maybe he did but it wasn't an unselfish love. He loved me as long as I did what he expected.

Would it change things between Ian and me? I told him I wanted casual. What right do I have to change the rules?

Why take a chance on ruining what we have?

His chest rises and falls in an even pattern. I glance up at his face. His eyes are closed. He's fallen asleep.

I pull a sheet over us and snuggle into his side.

I'll keep these feelings to myself for now. He said he ended one relationship because she wanted too much and he wasn't ready for it. I don't want to be lumped into the same category as his past relationships or, heaven help me, be compared to one of his brother's crazy ex-girlfriends.

CHAPTER 31

"*D*o you remember how Mom would always insist on telling us our birth stories on our birthdays?"

"Of course. I still do the same for Drew."

Rach sits on the couch and draws her legs up to her chest. "I used to find it so stupid and annoying she did that."

"Really? I always enjoyed hearing her tell it. Dad would chime in with his perspective about something silly. Like the doctor teasing her she was going to suck all the oxygen out of the room with her rapid breathing when she was delivering Drew."

She laughs. "Mom would always roll her eyes and say when you carry a baby inside you for nine months and spend a day in labor and have to push a nine-pound watermelon out of you, then you can tell the story the way you want."

"That was for you. For me, she would change it two days in labor and an eight-pound octopus. She said I wouldn't lie still and my arms and legs moved constantly."

"I'd give anything to hear her tell those stories again. It's nice you kept the tradition alive for Drew."

Rachelle came over and spent time with Drew after school and stayed for dinner. Drew went to bed and the two of us brought our glasses of wine into the living room and sat on the couch. Her mood had quieted over the course of the night. I thought she was just tired, but maybe there was more to it. I have my nostalgic melancholy moods too.

"Do you want to look at our old photo albums together?"

She glances up and grins. "Love to."

I rise and walk over to the cherrywood trunk I kept from my parents' house. All our old photo albums and memorabilia are inside. I haven't looked at them since we moved to Granite Cove and rarely before then—only when Drew insisted I look with him. Too painful to see the evidence of everything we lost and dredge up those feelings and memories. I thought it best to move on and not be stuck in the past. Maybe now that the three of us are together again I can remember the good without the pain.

The oldest set is showing its age with loose photos from disinte-grated adhesive. I grab the top ones from when Rachelle was born. The stack is heavy. I grimace. I need to start an exercise regimen and stick to it.

I sit next to Rachelle and open the first one across our laps. Baby pictures change over to pictures of her with her gap-toothed smile. She points and laughs at the pictures.

"I'd forgotten how prominent the gap was. Good thing Mom and Dad got me braces."

"You must have lost your retainer a dozen times."

"At least. Drove them nuts."

Pictures of our happy family span every page. We girls stand or sit with our arms around each other and grins on our faces with our parents beaming behind or next to us.

Drew arrives and the pictures continue with happy and laughing faces. I begin my role as babysitter and Rachelle's pictures morph into daredevil displays on top of boulders and hanging from trees.

"You were such a tomboy."

"You were Mom's little helper."

Her finger traces over a picture of just our parents, hugging and smiling for the camera. "They look so happy."

"I think they were."

"Don't you remember their loud arguments barely muffled by their bedroom door?"

I frown and think back. "No, I mean of course they had disagreements, but I don't remember a lot of them."

"I do. I guess you had already moved out and gone to college. They were mostly about Drew and all his diagnoses. Once he began school and his meltdowns exploded, they argued constantly."

"I knew they were concerned, but I didn't know they fought over it."

"Mom always wanted more testing, and Dad wanted to give Drew time to mature. Or they would argue about the medical bills."

"I'm sorry, I didn't know. That must have been stressful."

"It got so bad for a while I was sure they would get a divorce."

My mouth drops open. Could it really have been so bad and I not aware?

She shrugs. "It might have been my dramatic teenage brain."

I examine the pictures as we enter her teenage years. I'm in fewer of the photos as I've already left for college. The years pass by quicker as there are not as many photos documenting our lives. I hadn't noticed the lack before. Was it because the newness had worn off? Time became too precious, busy with more kids? Or had they really been unhappy and less inclined to immortalize the decline?

"You really think they were so unhappy?"

"At the time I did, but in hindsight, I think they were overwhelmed with making sure Drew had all the support he needed."

"You felt left out."

"Yeah, but I was a kid and I didn't understand what they had to deal with. I certainly didn't make it any easier on them, getting in trouble all the time."

She taps a picture of all of us in front of the Christmas tree. "We were still a happy family. We were a typical family with problems just like any other family. No family is perfect because people aren't perfect."

I bump her shoulder with mine. "That's a very mature observation."

"Took me longer than most, but I finally grew up."

"We all have our different paths." I run my finger over my parents' faces. This was the second-to-last Christmas we had together. "I never doubted for a minute they loved each other. I can't fathom they might have separated."

"I don't think they stopped loving each other. They were still affectionate with one another when they weren't fighting. Dad would kiss her, and she would give him that look and mumble under her breath..."

"'Not in front of the kids,'" we say at the same time and laugh.

"They were good people and excellent parents."

I nod. "Whenever I felt at a complete loss as to how to help Drew, I would ask myself what Mom or Dad would do. I asked myself that question many times in the beginning."

"You've done an amazing job with him, Becks. They would be so proud."

"I hope so."

We close the lid on the last photo album from while they were still alive.

"I'd like to see some photos from all the years I missed."

I carry the albums back to the chest. "I have to admit I haven't been as dedicated taking pictures." I pick up the photo books I've made over the years and carry them over. Instead of loose photos, each printed page has a couple or few photos with captions.

She laughs over pictures of Drew sticking his tongue out or putting on a goofy smile.

"He used to argue over having his picture taken even though he enjoys looking at the photos. You wouldn't believe how many shots I had to take just to get these instead of ones with him running away or putting his hands up to block the picture."

"I don't see any with any men in them, or anyone else for that matter. What about friends, boyfriends?"

"Other than the occasional picture of Jane, I doubt you'll find any." I shrug. "Relationships were hard and not my priority."

She closes the last book and sets it on the table and picks up her cup of tea. "What about Ian?"

I turn into the corner of the couch, prop my elbow on the back, and lean my head against my hand. "He's more of a recent addition, and I haven't made any photo books this year."

She sips at her tea and nods. "He's one of the good ones and there aren't many of them out there."

I lift my head from my hand. "Something you want to share?"

Rach hasn't mentioned any relationships. It's been eight years though. I'm sure there've been a few.

She frowns. "I just meant we all have had our experiences with rotten apples."

I roll my eyes. "That's for sure."

"He's a keeper. Don't let him get away."

I pluck a piece of lint off my jeans. "He's a human being. It's not like I can keep him locked up or anything. He has his own free will. It's not just up to me."

"But you want to keep him? You're in love with him, right? I've seen the way you look at each other."

I drop my head back and stare at the ceiling. "Why does everyone keep asking me about love?" I look back at her and sigh. "This isn't some fairy tale. I get why Franny and Olivia ask me since they're engaged or newlyweds and think love is all flowers and unicorns. What about you? Have you been in love?"

She cradles her cup in her hands and stares at the floor. "I thought I was, but it didn't work out."

Has someone hurt my little sister? I tense and drum my fingers on the back of the couch. "Do you want to talk about it?"

She smiles and shakes her head. "Maybe another time. It's ancient history. You haven't answered the question. Are you in love with him?"

I huff out a breath. "Yes."

She places her cup on the table and chuckles. "Doesn't sound like you want to be."

Do I? Why would anyone choose to be in love and suffer through all the indecision and insecurities? To be afraid and out of control? To wonder and guess what the other person is feeling?

I shake my head. "It's not what we agreed on. We said it would be casual. I feel like I'm breaking a contract or something by falling in love with him."

"I guess you haven't told him then, and he hasn't said it to you?"

I grab the pillow from behind me and put in my lap, wrapping my arms around it, and hugging it to my body. "No."

She purses her lips. "And you don't plan to?"

That's a definite no. "We're good where we are. I don't want to mess that up with declarations of love. When he's ready, he can tell me."

"So, you want him to say the words first?"

"Definitely."

She tucks her legs beneath her and snickers. "Never took you for a coward, Becks."

My mouth drops open, and I glare at her.

"It's not cowardly. Maybe self-preservation has something to do with it, but If I tell him I love him, then doesn't that put pressure on him to say it back? I know I felt pressured when Jeff said it to me first."

"Weren't you in love with Jeff? You planned to marry him. You were living with him when I left."

I wave my hand in the air. "I was young and naive and believed in happily ever after. Besides, our relationship was simple with no complications back then. When Mom and Dad died, he showed his true colors. He was definitely one of those rotten apples you mentioned."

She tilts her head and frowns. "You don't believe in happily ever after anymore? Do you really think only the young and naive fall in love?"

"I don't know if I believe in happily ever after. It's certainly a nice sentiment, but how realistic is it really? You know the divorce rate is ridiculously high. I'm neither young nor naive anymore. I feel twice my age most days."

She points a long finger at me. "Yet, you are in love. So, what do you think love is at your advanced age of thirty and with all your experience and wisdom?"

"Your sarcasm is duly noted. I think love is terrifying and a hell of a lot of work to make it last."

"Isn't it worth the hard work to have a partner in life who will stand by you and support you on those days you're feeling twice your age?"

I narrow my eyes. "When did you get so wise, little sister?"

"It's easy to give advice when you're talking about someone else's life. It's not so easy when it's your own."

"Ain't that the truth."

CHAPTER 32

"There are no orders or appointments today, so it will be just walk-ins. Remember, if you need me, call me."

"I got it." Cat gives me a tight smile.

Okay, I might have told her the same thing a few times already. "Sorry. I know you can take care of the shop in my absence."

"You're going to lunch, not on vacation. Who are you having lunch with anyway?"

"Ian's mother." I smooth my royal blue silk blouse over my abdomen and check the door for the dozenth time.

"Ooh, no wonder you're nervous. Do you get along with your boyfriend's mother?"

"I'm not nervous." *Much.* "She's a lovely woman. We get along wonderfully." *I think.*

I just wish I knew why she asked me to lunch. When she called and asked if I was free, of course I said yes, but then I began to wonder what she wanted to talk about. She might just be being friendly and want to get to know the woman her son is dating better. She might do this with all her sons' girlfriends.

Or she might want to tell me I'm not good enough for her precious son.

No, Molly isn't the type of woman to do that. She might think it, but she wouldn't invite me out to lunch to warn me off.

The bell over the door rings, and I whirl around. Molly walks in, smiling and dressed in wide-legged denim capris and a cute floral boxy top.

"Hi, there. Ready for lunch?"

"Yes, hello. I like your outfit."

She glances down. "Thanks. I felt like dressing up a little today instead of wearing what I call my farm clothes." She smiles. "You look lovely as always."

"Oh, thank you."

She glances over to Cat. "Hi, Catherine. How are your parents?"

"They're good. Mom's already decorating for Halloween. It's her favorite holiday."

My gaze darts between them. A curse or a perk of small towns? Most long-term residents have at least a passing acquaintance with the other long-termers. Maybe I should ask Cat what she knows later.

"Speaking of Halloween, remind me to get out our store decorations after lunch."

"Will do, boss. Enjoy your meal."

Molly and I step outside into the sunshine. The air is cooling as we get further into September, but the sun is still strong enough that we don't need jackets.

"I thought we'd have lunch outside on the patio at the inn since the weather is still so nice. Does that suit you?"

We turn right on the sidewalk. "I like the White Birch Inn. I haven't had a chance to enjoy the patio yet, so that sounds perfect." I glance up at the blue skies with a few white puffy clouds.

"Susan and I like to watch the boats go by on the lake while we have lunch there."

"Is she working at the hospital today?"

"Yes. She's working only part time now and has been talking about the possibility of retiring in a few years, but I don't believe a word of it. She loves being a nurse too much."

I chuckle. "It's good to do what you love, and we need more great nurses."

"She started out going to medical school to become a doctor but changed her mind and became a nurse instead because she wanted to spend more time with the patients. She's special. One of the many reasons I love her."

The inn is only a quarter of a mile from my shop. We pass by The Sweet Spot, and I peek in the window, but I see only a wall of customers.

"We should save room for dessert and pop into the bakery after lunch. They supply the inn with baked goods, but they have these little cheesecake bombs that are to die for."

I rest my hand on her arm. "They're a personal favorite of mine. Franny spoils me and brings them to the small business group meetings every month."

Molly shakes her head. "Silly me. I forgot she's your friend. Ian told me the wedding was something to see. Franny's mother and I have never been friendly—we run in different circles—but Franny is a sweet girl."

"She's the best."

The big white colonial sits on a hill at the corner of the cove. Wings have been added over the decades since it was turned from a private home into an inn. The restaurant occupies the original part in the center. A discreet plaque to the right of the entrance notes that the house is almost two centuries old.

Molly precedes me and tells the hostess behind the lectern in front of the open glass-filled double doors we wish to dine on the patio. I look over to the left and the check-in counter for guests of the inn. A woman smiles warmly at a couple. A small suitcase rests against the man's leg. It's early for leaf-peeping, but perhaps they're here for a romantic getaway.

"This way, please."

We follow the hostess through the restaurant to the gray stone patio, where an array of black metal tables and chairs with small white umbrellas wait. Only about half the tables are occupied. Beyond the short metal railing lies a green lawn which slopes down to the lake. A towering oak tree shades the lawn, and a metal bench curves around its base for guests to enjoy the view.

"Will this table suit?" The hostess stops at a table for two with an unobstructed view of the lake.

Molly glances at me.

"Yes, thank you."

The hostess hands us menus and lets us know our server will be with us shortly.

I skim the shortened lunch menu and quickly decide on the lobster bisque and the house salad. I set the menu down and look out at the lake while Molly studies her menu.

The lake is busy, with people trying to squeeze in the last few good boating days before the weather turns cold.

"Have you decided?"

"Lobster bisque and a salad. You?"

"I'm partial to their crab cakes. Would you like to split an order?"

"None for me, thanks."

"In that case, I think I'll order those and the scallops. Two appetizers for my meal. Do you think I'm being gluttonous?"

"Hardly. You haven't seen Drew devour an entire pizza on his own."

"Ah, well, he's a growing boy, and they're never full."

The server takes our orders and silently disappears.

"I gather Ian told you about Conner's girlfriend?"

"He told me Conner broke up with her and she wasn't accepting it well. Has she caused more problems?"

"Mike told me yesterday she tried to file a restraining order against Conner, saying he was threatening her."

"That's awful. What did he do?"

"Luckily, the police did their due diligence. She's done this before apparently, and it's the boyfriends that ended up filing restraining orders against her. Which Conner finally did." She shakes her head. "To think she's been to my house and I never once suspected she was capable of such deviousness. I can't say I thought she was right for him, but I didn't see this."

"I only met her the one time at the July fourth picnic, but it's hard to know someone and what they're capable of after a couple meetings."

"I don't know. I think some people you just know are good or not so good right away."

She glances out at the lake. "A mother only wants her child to be happy. I never push any of my sons toward someone or away from them. The heart chooses who to love. What I think doesn't matter."

I bite my lower lip. "Molly, I realize I'm probably not your choice for Ian either. I come with a lot of baggage."

She tilts her head and studies me. "Curious that you would think that. Have I said or done something to make you feel that way?"

"No, not at all. You've been kind and welcoming. I just can't help but make the leap in my head when you invite me to lunch out of the blue and then talk about your sons' girlfriends."

"Life is how you choose to look at it. Find the positive in each moment. If you focus on the negative, it becomes a self-fulfilling prophecy."

"I'm a worrier. I guess I've become a glass-half-empty person."

The server fills my water and delivers Molly's iced tea.

"There's always time to change your perspective."

"I suppose you're right."

She sighs and lays her hands in her lap. "My sons are very different from each other. They all share certain similarities, of course. They're brothers and were raised the same way. But they each have their own quirks, if you will, especially when it comes to their romantic relationships. Mike likes his life comfortable. He takes a long time to make a decision, and he's not a fan of change. His relationships have always been long term. I think the shortest was two years. Conner is more of a serial dater. He has relationships, but they turn over rather quickly. And, as you've witnessed, he gravitates toward drama."

I sip my water and nod. I can see this about both of them. I spin my mother's ring on my finger. What about Ian? What kind of dater is he?

She rests her elbows on the table, folds her hands together, and sets her chin on them as she gazes over at me. "Then there are my twins. Neither one of them reveal much about their love lives to me. I have to be sneakier about getting information. I know Ian dates. We live in the same small town. It's not easy to keep those types of secrets. Ryan doesn't live here, so I know nothing."

Don't care about Ryan. Tell me more about Ian.

My mother's ring circles my finger around and around. I probably should get it resized to fit my finger properly, but what if something happened to it at the jeweler's?

"They both had girls calling them in high school. Ian had girl-friends, but none of them lasted long." She shrugs. "He was in high school. I wasn't concerned. He went to college, so I didn't see him daily." She glances at me as she sips her iced tea. "That was hard. I like my boys close. I go into withdrawal if I don't talk to them on a regular basis."

Ian's family is very close. It's easy to see the love they have for each other every time I see them together.

"Understandable."

The server arrives with our food, and I impatiently wait for Molly to continue her story. I practically snatch my salad out of the server's hands.

"This looks delicious." She turns each plate in front of her and leans over and inhales.

Please don't stop now. You can eat later.

She unfolds the napkin and lays it in her lap. I snap mine and drop it haphazardly in my lap.

"Being the nosy mother that I am, I would ask him about any women he was seeing. Occasionally he would mention a woman's name and say they were dating. When I would ask about her later on, the names often changed. Again, college, so I wasn't overly concerned."

She cuts one of the crab cakes into quarters and takes a bite.

There has to be a reason she's telling me all this, right?

Good Lord! What if she's about to tell me Ian had met his soulmate or something? Ian had glossed over his past relationships. Maybe there's a reason for that.

"As the years passed, he moved back to Granite Cove and opened Flannigan's Pub. When he dated a woman and they ultimately parted ways, I would go over to his apartment—he was living in the attic of his pub then. I'd bring his comfort foods from childhood: lasagna or this rice casserole I make." She waves her fingers in the air and takes a bite of her scallops. "Anyway, each and every time I would do this, he would laugh and say he was fine. At first, I thought maybe it was some macho thing to deny hurt feelings or something. But I soon realized it wasn't that at all. He was fine and not hurt. He hadn't cared enough about any of them to be hurt. He wasn't in love."

Okay, that lines up with what he told me. Where is she going with this? And can she get there any faster?

"Aren't you going to eat?"

I look down at my bisque and salad. I'd probably choke if I tried.

I stir the bisque. "I'm letting it cool."

"A couple of years ago, Ian announced he'd bought property in town and wanted Mike to design a house for him. I thought, why now? Could there be a special someone finally? Then I began to hear whispers of Ian and this new woman in town."

Me? She is talking about me, right? Wait, is she saying I'm the reason Ian decided to build a house? No, the timing is off. I only moved to Granite Cove less than two years ago. Our one-night stand was about two years ago, but that doesn't make sense.

She glances at me over the tops of her glasses. "My curiosity brought me to your store a few times, and I would listen closely every time someone mentioned the new florist in town."

She is *talking about me.* My face grows hot. I glance up at the open umbrella. Am I sitting directly in the sun?

"Have some water. You look flushed."

I guzzle half the glass as she takes a bite of each of her dishes.

I watch her chew each mouthful thoroughly with a slight smile on her face.

My gaze narrows, and I look up at her smiling, innocent face.

"You're enjoying this, aren't you?"

"A little."

"Ugh!" I drop my head on the back of the chair and stare up at the blue sky. My brain is spinning with so many questions.

I look back at her calmly eating her meal.

"What exactly are you implying? I need it in plain words. Because my brain is jumping to too many conclusions."

She lays her fork down and folds her hands together on the table in front of her plate. "Since the whispers about you and Ian started, I've seen him frustrated, confused, and downright irritated. But I've also seen him happy, engaged, peaceful. He's finally talking to his family about his love life. Ian finally cares."

Well, shit! My eyes fill, but I bite my tongue and stare at the lake until they fade away.

"Would you like to hear what I discovered about you while I did my reconnaissance?"

I snort and rub the space between my eyes. "I'm not entirely sure."

She chuckles. "Many mentioned your beauty, but I could see that for myself and it didn't interest me. Beauty fades. I wanted to know what kind of woman you were. Professional, smart, driven, friendly but reserved...these were all used more than once. I had the outer frame of the jigsaw puzzle forming, but the center—the hard part—was still empty."

"Then I met you for myself. The pieces all fit together beautifully, and I had a complete picture of a woman who not only knew how to love, but one who, when she gave her heart, would give it completely and do anything to ensure that person's happiness. That is a woman I am very proud to see with my son."

Tears fill and spill over my eyes and down my cheeks. I lower my head and use my napkin to hide my loss of control.

A scraping screech sounds as Molly scoots her chair around the table to hug me. "There's nothing wrong with tears, Rebecca. I cry all the time, but the tears of happiness are the best. These are happy tears, aren't they? I'd feel awful if I said something to upset you."

I nod silently as I sniffle into my napkin.

She rubs my arm. "Good. Let them out."

Ian cares for me, and he just might return my love.

And his mom thinks I'm wonderful.

Can't get much better than that. Why can't I stop crying? I'm making a complete spectacle of myself.

"If he does love me, why hasn't he told me?"

"Interesting question. Have you told him?"

I jerk my head up. Did I say that out loud?

She stares at me with a smile on her face and her arm still wrapped around me.

"I, um…well, no. I thought it might put pressure on him to say it back, and I don't want him to say it because he feels obligated to."

"Rebecca, my son has been chasing after you for over a year. Do you know each time the family has gotten together he's lectured us beforehand not to scare you away?"

"He did? Why? You're all wonderful."

She laughs and scoots her chair back. "Thank you. I think my family is pretty wonderful, too, but I'm biased. Now I need to eat this food before it gets cold, so forgive me if I continue talking with my mouth full."

"No, please, go ahead."

She does but points to my food with her fork while she chews.

I pick up my spoon and stir the bisque.

"Ian has confided some of your history to me, and I know about your deal to be bed buddies."

Oh Lord!

I cover my eyes with my hand. How could he tell his mother that?

"There's nothing to be embarrassed about. Sex is a perfectly natural bodily function. God designed us this way. People get uptight about the silliest things."

"You're my boyfriend's mother. It's not a conversation I expected to have."

"Why not? I've talked with both Steve's and Susan's mothers about sex before."

"I guess I'm not as evolved as you are then. I suppose it is societal and cultural convention that makes it seem awkward. I should try to do better. Probably why I'm having such a tough time figuring out how to have the talk with Drew."

"If you're nervous and uncomfortable about sex, he'll think it's something wrong rather than something beautiful."

"Good point."

My brain is fuzzy. I feel like I'm walking through a thick fog searching for answers, but they're playing hide and seek. Is she right about Ian? Does he love me too? Should I tell him how I feel? What if she's wrong?

I sip at my bisque, probably cold by now.

It's creamy and delicious. It could be warmer, but it's not ruined by my neglect.

Molly finishes her lunch and stacks her dishes together on the edge of the table. "You, more than most, know the value of time. You can lose someone in an instant. Don't waste whatever precious time you have. Tell him how you feel. Put yourself out there. It's your turn to do some of the chasing. Although I'm confident Ian won't be running anywhere but toward you."

CHAPTER 33

The oven is on and preheating. The lasagna is on the counter and ready to go in the oven. Thank God, I made it yesterday so I wouldn't have to worry about cooking anything complicated today. It's hard to mess up a lasagna, and Molly said it was one of Ian's favorites.

Ian should be here soon. He'll be surprised when he finds a romantic dinner for two instead of the pizza night with Drew he expects.

I smooth the front of my new little black dress as I glance over the set table and the candles ready to be lit. He will see it as soon as he enters.

I haven't used the table in so long, the flaps were stuck. I had to wrestle them open after I dragged it into the center of the room.

My phone rings with Ian's own special bluesy ringtone. I should have known when I programmed my phone to play a special ringtone that I was falling for him. No one else except my brother and now my sister have one.

"Hi."

"Hey, I hate to do this, but is there any chance you and Drew can come to my house for dinner? My battery in my Jeep died. I'm charging it, but I think I need a new one, and even if I don't, it'll take a while to charge. We can order a pizza and have it delivered."

My gaze darts around my apartment. Should I cancel?

"Rebecca?"

"Um, yeah, of course. It'll be a few minutes."

"No problem. I want to jump in the shower anyway after working on the Jeep. I'll leave the door unlocked for you guys."

"Perfect."

"See you soon, beautiful."

I close my eyes as the phone disconnects. Do I take the lasagna over there and try to salvage the evening or scrap it and wait for another night to confess my love?

Screw it. I'm not getting myself all worked up over this a second time. I cover the lasagna and put it in a tote, shut off the oven, and stuff the salads I made and the Italian bread I bought into the tote too.

I dart out of the kitchen to the romantic table I prepared and shift from one foot to the other. I can take the candles and the fresh flower arrangement I made, but should I take the rest or scrounge his kitchen for the replacements?

Best to take everything. That way I know I'll be prepared and not have to panic.

I pack an overnight bag just in case and load the car.

I'm salvaging this night no matter what the universe throws at me. I stop in my tracks as I open the driver's door and glare up at the sky. "That was not a dare."

His door is unlocked as promised when I arrive. I carry everything into his kitchen while peeking toward his upstairs and listening for any sound from him. His oven is a modern sleek machine with controls that befuddle me for a few minutes. I finally get it turned on and preheating. I slide the lasagna in. I don't have time to wait for it to preheat. It's a convection oven. I search the internet for how long the lasagna should bake. At least we won't have to wait too long for dinner.

I arrange the flowers, candles, and place settings on his long glass table. The bedroom door opens with a click just as I step toward the kitchen to unpack the salads. Should I wait until he comes down?

I step back in front of the table and pose with a hand on my hip. This should send the message this is a romantic evening for two. I glance down at the slight hint of cleavage. Should I expose a little more?

No, we need to have dinner and conversation first, not go straight to bed.

His hair is wet and combed back as he waltzes into the kitchen in black joggers and a black T-shirt. His gaze skims over me and then the table behind me, and he halts halfway across the kitchen.

He glances around. "Where's Drew?"

"At Rachelle's."

A slow grin spreads over his full lips.

"I thought it would be nice to have dinner just the two of us tonight."

"You have my full approval, but I feel underdressed. Should I go up and change?"

"No."

He walks over to stand in front of me. "You sure?"

"I'm sure."

"You look amazing, sweetheart." He kisses me. With my three-inch heels I don't even have to stretch to wrap my arms around his neck and return his kiss.

He settles his hands on my hips and peers over my shoulder at the table. "You brought all this?" He glances behind him to the kitchen. "What do I smell? Italian?"

"Yes, lasagna."

"You cooked for me?"

"Don't act so surprised. It's not the first time."

"No, but it is the first time you've got flowers and candles. Are you trying to seduce me? You should know I'm a sure thing by now."

I laugh and playfully swat him on the shoulder. "I'm trying to be romantic. I suppose it seems rather silly."

"Not a bit. I'm touched. I'm going to have to up my game to show my appreciation."

He rests his linked hands at the small of my back.

"We should eat. I brought wine, salads, and bread. The lasagna won't take too long to bake."

"What can I do?"

"Sit. Everything is ready."

I pour us each a glass of wine and set salads at our settings. The bread is in a basket in the center.

He raises his glass. "To a wonderful surprise dinner with a beautiful woman."

I take a large gulp of wine. My original plan was to fill his belly with good food and then steer the conversation to all the things he's brought into my life that I'm thankful for. Finally, I'd tell him I love him. But the way my stomach is churning, I don't know if I can do it. Besides, it's not Thanksgiving, where we declare what we're thankful for. It sounds too cliché.

"Something wrong with your salad? Mine's great. What's this dressing? It's delicious."

"It's a champagne vinaigrette."

He takes another bite while I drink more wine.

"Ian?"

He glances up.

"Thank you for not giving up on me."

He sets his fork down.

I shove my chair back and jump up.

He starts to stand.

I throw up a hand. "Wait. I thought I had this all planned out, but then you called so I had to improvise, and everything I thought to say now doesn't sound right." I pace behind my chair as I throw my hands up.

I spin around and face him. "I love you."

I sigh and rest my hands on top of the chair. There, I said it.

He stands and stalks down the length of the table.

I drop my hands from the chair and back up a few steps. "I didn't say that to pressure you into anything. You don't have to say it back."

He gives me a speaking look and yanks me into his arms. He devours my lips.

He lifts his head and rests his forehead against mine with our noses touching. His hands cup my face.

"I love you with every breath of my body and to the depths of my soul."

I blink. "Wow! You're better at this than I am."

He throws his head back and laughs.

He clasps my hand. "Come with me." He tugs me across the kitchen to the stairs.

"What? Wait. No, Ian. The lasagna will be ruined. We can't go upstairs."

"This will only take a few minutes. The lasagna will be fine."

I frown at his back as we climb the stairs. "You realize that's not exactly a ringing endorsement of your prowess in the bedroom, right?"

He snorts out a burst of laughter and pulls me across his bedroom to a dresser against the wall. He opens the top drawer and fishes something out with his free hand.

"What are you doing?"

"I had something different planned on your birthday, but I don't want to wait until November." He opens his hand to reveal a small jewelry box.

My gaze flies up to his. He said birthday. He must mean earrings or something.

"I bought this almost two months ago when I accepted the fact that I don't want to imagine a life without you in it." He opens the lid.

A diamond solitaire ring is nestled inside the black velvet. A marquise diamond. A rather large one.

My body feels like it's supported by jelly, not bones. Is he asking me to marry him?

"I think I've loved you since that night in Boston. I couldn't get you out of my head. When I built this house, I found myself picturing you inside it before you ever moved to Granite Cove. No matter how many times you turned me down, I couldn't make myself give up. Do you understand how rare that is for me? I've never had a problem forgetting a woman in my life. I began to believe I wasn't capable of falling in love before you."

I put my fingers over my lips as tears pour down my face.

He wipes the tears from my skin with the back of his fingers and takes my hand in his.

"The more I got to know you, the more I knew we were meant to be together. No two people could fit together as well as we did and not be destined for each other. The more you let me into your life, the more convinced I became. I was determined to take it slow and not spook you in to running again. I love you, Rebecca. Will you marry me?"

I drop his hand, bend over, and prop my hands on my knees. There's a ringing in my ears. My chest is tight, like all the air is being sucked out of the room. I gasp and concentrate on breathing in and out.

Ian wraps an arm around me.

I fall against the support and warmth of his body.

He asked me to marry him!

I take a deep breath and rise, leaning on him heavily. *Get it together, Rebecca.*

I chew on my lip. "I thought you might say you loved me back. I didn't expect this."

"Is that good or bad?"

The ring sparkles in his hand.

"Rebecca?" He bends his head and searches my face. "Too much?"

I step away from him and cup my cheeks in my palms. "No... I mean not no *no*, as in no to the proposal. I mean... Jesus, I don't know what I mean. You've jumped a dozen steps ahead of me. I need a minute to wrap my brain around this and catch up."

I pinch the bridge of my nose and pace back and forth, staring at the ring still in his hand.

"I thought we'd confess our love and I don't know...continue to say it until we were both comfortable saying and hearing the words? Feeling the words? Marriage didn't cross my mind except in some abstract future possibility."

I stop and drag my gaze from the ring to his face. "Have you thought this through? Do you understand what marriage to me involves?"

"Are you talking about Drew or your need for everything to follow a logical order of things you can manage with your mountain of lists?"

"You're trying to be funny?"

He smirks. "I thought you might need a little levity."

I close my eyes and sigh.

He pulls me to him by my waist and clasps his hands behind me. "Baby, you're overthinking this. I love you. You love me. Nothing else matters. We'll figure it out. I know you and Drew are a package deal."

"Yes, but do you understand it could be forever? I don't know if he'll ever be independent enough to live on his own."

"Then we'll build him an apartment in the basement. It has plenty of space and a walkout sliding door."

I smash my lips together as tears fill my eyes.

I place my hands on his cheeks. "Thank you. You're a wonderful man. I love you so much."

He kisses the tears streaming down my face. "You're my world, and now Drew is too. I would never try to cut him out of it in any way. Your family is my family, just like mine is yours. Are you ready to take my family on? That's probably the bigger question. There's a lot more of them."

"I love your family, especially your mother. Did she tell you about our lunch?"

"You had lunch with my mother?"

I nod. "She likes me."

"She loves you."

He rests his forehead against mine. "If you're not ready to get married, we can wait. Or have a long engagement."

"No."

"No... No wedding or no engagement? I need a little more detail here."

"No, I don't want to wait."

He grins. "Yeah?"

"Yeah, let me see that giant ring again."

Ian chuckles and pulls it out of his pocket. "If you don't like it, we can get something else."

"No, I want this one. I love it." I scrub my cheeks and hope I don't have makeup streaked all over my face like some clown from a horror film. "Ask me again."

He holds my left hand in his. "Rebecca Terrance, will you do me the honor of becoming my wife?"

I nod enthusiastically. "Yes."

He slips the engagement ring onto my ring finger.

"Oh crap! Here go the waterworks again." Tears flow freely as Ian kisses each of my hands and then my lips.

His cheeks are wet. I open my eyes and stare at the tracks of tears on his face.

"I love you, you big softy."

"A man's tears are a sign of his emotional maturity."

I laugh. "Oh, yeah? Did your mother tell you that?"

"She may have. Are you going to disagree with my mother?"

"Never."

The peel of the smoke alarm system fills the house as one unit after another shrieks in a warped chorus.

The lasagna!

EPILOGUE

*C*ool sand squishes between my bare toes. Water gently laps at the shore a few feet away. The sun is a golden ball of fire sinking toward the horizon. Ribbons of lavender and pink flow through the evening sky.

Ian's hands clasp mine between us. His beautiful sea-blue eyes sparkle down at me. The points of his white button-down shirt flap in the breeze. His black pants are cuffed above his ankles, and sand sprinkles his bare feet.

Drew stands behind him with a giant grin on his face. Rach stands next to him, discreetly wiping tears from her cheeks. I smile at them both.

Franny and Mitch stand with their arms around each other, and Olivia stands next to them with Luke behind her. His arms are folded over her waist. Kelly, Kerry, and Lucinda complete the semi-circle behind Ian.

The justice of the peace asks for the rings, and Ryan steps next to my shoulder, holding them out. There are a few sniffles behind me. I can only guess they're coming from Molly and Rose.

Ian takes my wedding ring and holds it at the tip of my finger.

"With this ring, I wed the love of my life. The most beautiful woman inside and out I've ever laid eyes on. The powerful woman with the marshmallow center. The woman I can't wait to spend the rest of my days thanking my lucky stars I found. I love you, killer." The ring is warm from his touch as he slides it over my finger.

I close my eyes and laugh. Of course he would throw that dratted nickname in.

The justice of the peace hands me Ian's wedding ring. My hand shakes as I hold it in front of his. Ian chuckles and gives my other hand a squeeze.

"With this ring, I wed the most persistent man I've ever had the greatest fortune to meet." Chuckles come from all around. "I begin each day in gratitude for his tenacious pursuit. You showed me the possibilities of love. You taught me to trust in that love. I treasure the day the universe sent you to me, and I promise to love you with all of my heart every day of our lives."

"I now pronounce you husband and wife. You..."

Drew claps with all his strength like a machine gun of slapping skin.

We all laugh, and the justice of the peace finishes his proclamation. "You may kiss the bride."

Our lips meet, but we're both grinning too hard to manage much more than a brush of lips.

Ian's family cheers behind me, and both sides rush forward to engulf us in hugs and kisses.

Lucinda rocks me side to side with tears filling her eyes. "Such beautiful, simplistic perfection."

"I couldn't have done it without you." She threw together this wedding on the beach in front of Ian's house in two weeks' time. Our house. Drew and I moved in last week.

She shakes her head. "I didn't do anything. You two are what made it so beautiful. Just your love, family, friends, and the sunset on the beach."

Molly clasps my cheeks in her hands and kisses me. "Welcome to the family!"

"Hey, do I get to kiss her too?" Ryan leans his head over my shoulder.

"Get your own girl." Ian puts his arm around my shoulders.

"Let's go back to the house and celebrate. There's a pile of food waiting for us," Susan says.

The group of us walk hand in hand down the path to the house. Drew laughs as Mike and Ryan joke with him in front of us.

Lights strung all over the backyard glow like fireflies and fairies waltzing beneath the stars. The tables pushed together form one long line with white tablecloths hanging low and place settings of gold. Short, fat vases filled with pink mums, white roses, and peach tulips line the center. The flames of the ivory candles shine like beacons of hope.

Love blossoms in my chest and overflows my spirit. I swear I can feel Mom and Dad watching and smiling while Ian kisses the back of my hand and our friends and family sit around us.

READ FRANNY'S STORY, My First My Last My Only

READ OLIVIA'S STORY, Covet thy Neighbor

SIGN up for my Newsletter to be the first to hear about new releases, sales, giveaways, and exclusive content.

THANK YOU FOR READING!

ACKNOWLEDGMENTS

This book is especially close to my heart because the character, Drew is inspired by my son, Jared. He has many of the same diagnoses, including autism. I do not intend for my presentation of Drew to be representative of all those on the autism spectrum.

ABOUT THE AUTHOR

Denise Carbo writes Contemporary Romance, Paranormal Romance, and Romantic Suspense. She is a voracious reader, loves to travel, is fascinated by the supernatural, and enjoys solving mysteries.

She lives in a small, picturesque New England town with her high school sweetheart and their three amazing sons. Find out more at https://www.DeniseCarbo.com and sign up for her newsletter to be the first to hear about new releases, sales, giveaways, contests, and exclusive content. https://eepurl.com/dt5N7M

ALSO BY DENISE CARBO

My First My Last My Only
Covet thy Neighbor

Made in the USA
Columbia, SC
11 May 2022

60292315R00122